Dedication

To Owen Sutherland and all members of

U3A Moraira – Teulada Creative Writing Group,

Past and Present.

With a special mention to Geoffrey Shean,

a wonderful inspiration and greatly missed.

All Rights Reserved

First published 2018

ISBN: 9781726653084

About Our Group

In 2008 a group of people formed the Moraira – Teulada U3A and shortly after its inauguration various groups were organised, including the Creative Writing Group.

Now, in 2018 - our 10th Anniversary year - we want to celebrate all the stories that have been written during that time, over 2,000 of them, by creating a small memento that hopefully will be enjoyed by many and also raise some much needed funds for our chosen local charity.

We thought it important to have a common theme running through the book that would hold the attention of you, the reader and also show the eclectic mix of work from the current authors within our group – hence the title "Lucky Escapes".

We hope that you enjoy the many twists and turns that this subject evokes.

"Make A Smile" Charity

Every year Moraira – Teulada U3A
adopt a local charity, "Make A Smile" is the chosen
local charity for 2018 and we hope you will
support them in as many ways as you are able,
including buying this book, of course, and all profits
will be donated to them.

For more information on "Make A Smile" Charity
please look at their website - http://makeasmile.es/

CONTENTS

JACK'S TALE

BY DOT GARRETT

I awake to a sudden loud noise and for a few minutes wonder where I am. This is not my bed. My senses are on high alert and suddenly I feel flooded with strange smells, musky and damp.

It is dark, not just of the night but also the closed in darkness of four walls. There are no windows. Fear surrounds me and seeps into every pore and I am shivering with cold and apprehension.

As I gradually come to and try to stretch and yawn in the small cramped space that is mine I wonder how long I have been here now and, more importantly, how much longer I have to stay. What will become of me? Where is my family? I don't know why I am here and no one will tell me. Memories of my family and playing with the children force their way into my mind and sadness threatens to engulf me. I want to cry out but try desperately to suppress it, unsure if I will be punished.

I wonder how long it will be until my captors come to release me for the short time I am allowed for exercise and toilet needs. Oh no! Now I have thought of going to the toilet I have a desperate need to pee! I pace the small space and try desperately to think of something else. When I first arrived here I had a couple of accidents. The man came and he said I was bad but the other one, the woman, she seemed to understand, her voice was softer but I felt so ashamed. They didn't punish me but I have tried not to let it happen again. Not knowing if they will turn nasty is fear enough.

Finally I hear the footsteps approaching that herald my short release into the open area. The relief is enormous and I am fidgeting with impatience.

It's the woman today; perhaps this is a good omen. I clutch at straws but I am still afraid to look into her eyes, will I see hope or pity?

As she releases me into the outside compound I head straight to the toilets, the relief is palpable! Then I do a couple of laps of the yard. I am breathing deeply as the fresh air is like an aphrodisiac to my senses.

All too soon I have to return to my cell. I feel the rumblings of hunger and eagerly await the arrival of breakfast and fresh water. The food is edible but not what I am used to. Although I found it hard to eat upon my arrival I have now accepted that I need to keep my strength up. The day stretches uneventfully before me.

After breakfast I feel I might as well try and sleep for a while and rearrange the small amount of bedding I have but it is impossible to make it any more comfortable. I must have dozed off for a while. I am dreaming of the bright open space of home and friendly loving faces.

Suddenly I hear my name called, "Jack, are you there Jack?"
Am I still dreaming? I dare to hope.

Suddenly they are there, my family. The cell door opens and I rush out into their waiting arms. Joy threatens to overwhelm me now and I am shaking with ecstasy.

"Oh Jack, we are back, we missed you while we were on holiday" says my mistress and she kneels down to stroke me.

I lick the tears from her face and my tail won't stop wagging.

Note: I wrote this as a challenge when our group was invited to submit stories for a competition. Part of the remit was it had to be 500 words! I wondered about a dog's emotions and felt comparisons could be drawn with anyone finding themselves helpless and not understanding either the situation or language: a fear of the unknown. I was very pleased to be shortlisted and even more pleased when another in our group won the competition. That story is also to found in this book.

THE TIME MACHINE

BY JENNIFER NESTEROFF

Farmer George Simpson stomped into the farmhouse kitchen and remarked to his wife, who was in the middle of making jam, "Guess what our genius son is doing?"

His wife glared at him, "Now, you go back to the door and take those dirty gum-boots off before I listen to anything you say."

George did as he was told. "Sorry love, I was in a hurry to tell you about this latest stunt of his."

Margaret Simpson sighed. "Well, what is he doing now?"

"He's in the barn building a time machine, the daft rabbit!"

"A time machine, some sort of clock is it?"

Oh no! It's one of those contraptions that can take you to the future or back to the past if you've a mind to go to such places. He says he's been reading stories about time machines and reckons he's thought up great ideas for building one."

"Oh well, you never know, he's a bright lad really. You know how good he was at fixing the tractor after you ran it into that ditch and clogged up the thingamajig and broke the what-sit. He mended my sewing machine too and he's always tinkering about with the old truck; got it going when you said it was finished."

"Now you're being daft." George shook his head disapprovingly. "Trucks and tractors are one thing but I'd say building a time machine would be a tad trickier. You can't stick up for that lad of yours all the time."

"Perhaps not, but you've got to encourage children in all their little aspirations. Bill is a good boy and I'm sure he'll make a wonderful farmer one day."

George grunted. "Bill is thirty two, Margaret. It would be nice if he were a wonderful farmer now instead of playing around with all this mechanical stuff. All I can say is if he does get his time machine going, ha ha, he'd better have milked the cows before he goes flying off to other times!"

Secretly, Margaret Simpson was proud of what she thought of as her son's inventive abilities and she was quick to impress her lady friends with his latest project. The local Country Fair, at which she expected her entry of strawberry jam to win first prize in the cooking competition, was the perfect opportunity to spread the word. In fact, she was already planning to invite selected guests to witness the inaugural flight if and when it took place. Perhaps she could persuade Bill to get their neighbour, Irene Smith, nosy old cow, to go with him to some distant past or future and neglect to bring her back.

After several weeks Bill announced that he believed his invention was ready to be tested. By this time the whole community had heard about the project and the selected guests were joined by a hoard of uninvited individuals all anxious to behold the spectacle and hopefully get a good laugh out of it. Such is the uncharitable nature of many.

The local newspaper reporter was on the scene looking for a story that would, at least, make a change from the usual uninspiring events around the village.

Everyone gathered outside the barn doors waiting for Bill to open them. When he did they all crowded in and gazed at the long anticipated machine. There it stood, a large, rather ordinary looking wooden box with a door on one side which Bill opened so that they could inspect the interior. They saw a seat in front of which stood a panel of shiny buttons and a couple of leavers.

Irene Smith immediately stepped inside for a closer look. "What happens if I pull this leaver?" she inquired, reaching out to take hold of it.

"Don't touch that!" shouted Bill. "You wouldn't want to find yourself somewhere in the Middle Ages being tried as a witch, now would you?"

"Oh, go on, let her pull it!" thought Margaret, but didn't say.

People were getting very excited.

"Are you going to take it up now, Bill?" several asked

"Well, it doesn't actually go anywhere." Bill explained. "When I manipulate the right controls the machine will send me off on my journey and will wait here ready to receive me when I contact it with this to say I want to come back."

He produced a small object from his pocket that had the appearance of a television remote control.

"I've got one like that." remarked someone in the crowd.

"So have I!" exclaimed another.

"I think you'll find it's not the same as this," Bill said, using a quiet but mysterious tone.

"God give me strength," murmured George, who had been standing at the back. He shook his head and wandered off to visit his cows.

"Good, I'll be off then," said Bill. "Oh, there is just one thing I would ask all of you, you too Mum. Please do not go inside the machine while I am away. It must stay in good working order to enable it to bring me back."

Margaret rushed forward to give him a good-bye hug. "Don't worry Son, no one is going to get near it, I promise you!"

With a wave of his hand, Bill entered the box and closed the door. Soon a low humming sound could be heard followed by a loud whoosh. Then all was silent.

Everyone stood mesmerised for a few minutes until someone suggested they should take a peek inside to see what was going on. A discussion followed concerning the wisdom of doing so which was cut short when Irene Smith strode over and threw open the machine's door. They all gasped, the box was empty! There was no sign of Bill.

There was much animated chatter for the next couple of hours but eventually people became bored with hanging around and they all went home.

On a balmy summer evening, just as George and Margaret were sitting down to tea, they heard the sound of a car pulling into the farmyard. Looking through the window they were amazed to see a very smart BMW coming to a halt. Its door opened and out stepped Bill, looking very dapper in a tailored suit. Margaret jumped up and ran out to great him, followed more slowly by George.

"You're back from your travels at last! Where have you been and what exciting things happened to you?" Margaret cried with joy.

"I haven't been too far away Mum, just to the city to take up a job."

"So there was no time travel nonsense after all?" said George

"No Dad."

"Thought as much, I'm the only one with any sense around here, though it looks like you seem to have a pretty good head on your shoulders, too. What's been going on?"

"Well Dad, I just needed to see if I could make a go of doing something I really wanted to before I let you know, so I applied for a job with a big electronics company and went for an interview. They seemed to think I was a bit of a whiz kid and employed me straight away. I've been doing rather well ever since."

"Oh Bill! How clever you are." gushed Margaret. "Just wait till I tell everyone!"

Bill turned to George "By the way Dad, I've ordered you a good milking machine to make things easier for you. I'm afraid I don't want to go near another cow as long as I live."

"That's all right Son, so long as you're doing so well. Nice car, that. Just tell me, how did you manage to disappear from that so called time machine of yours?"

"Smoke and mirrors, Dad, just smoke and mirrors."

BAD SEX

BY ROSEMARY SHEPPARD

"But why does he have to come round at the same time every Thursday afternoon?" asked Edith, standing in the doorway to the kitchen where I was busily making scones.

"He enjoys my cooking," I replied, barely managing to conceal my irritation. Edith asked me the same question every Thursday morning and after a year of it I was beginning to get a little exasperated.

"Anyway," I continued, "I don't see why you need to get your knickers in a twist over it seeing as you're always upstairs having your nap when he's here and never even see him." I pounded the dough on the table a little more robustly than the recipe called for. It saved me having to go over and land one on Edith, which I felt like doing.

"I do wish you didn't feel that you had to use those vulgar expressions," she complained, touching her head with her hand as though I had actually hit her. She's ten years older than me, nearly seventy, and never married, never known a man in the biblical sense so she's had what one might call a sheltered existence. I, on the other hand, while I may be sixty have more than made up for her lack of experience, having been married twice and had more than my fair share of male company, hence the real reason for the vicar coming round every Thursday afternoon. It's not just my cooking which he enjoys.

"What vulgar expression was that, then?" I countered, knowing full well what she meant.

"About, um, knickers……" Her voice trailed away. Really, my sister seems to be getting more ridiculous every day and I told her so. Anyone would think we lived in a convent though I don't suppose the vicar would have been visiting a convent quite as regularly as he frequented our drawing room – oh, I don't know though. I've heard stories that, but no, I digress.

"I just don't understand what you find to talk about," she went on, looking very puzzled as she regularly did, every Thursday morning.

"Well, we manage," I replied thinking to myself that in fact there wasn't a lot of talking involved in our encounters. We just get on with it, if you see what I mean.

"It's not as though you've ever been religious," she continued.

"No, well, there are more things on earth etc. etc. etc.," I said, putting the scones onto a tray ready for baking. The vicar likes them with lots of raspberry jam, and plenty of cream. There always has to be plenty of cream.

"If you want me, I shall be in my room, doing my needlepoint." Edith is actually quite adept at things like that and is a member of the village sewing circle which she regularly attends.

"OK, dear! I'll see you later then. I thought we might have chicken for dinner."

"That will be most satisfactory," she replied over her shoulder as she left the room and went upstairs to her domain.

I popped the scones into the oven and started to get myself ready for the arrival of the vicar. Thinking back, I recalled how we had first met, at a social in the village hall, shortly after his arrival, which had in itself caused quite a stir at the time. The previous vicar had been almost as old as the god he worshipped, when he remembered to turn up at the church at all that is. Many had been the times when the congregation had found itself sitting in the hallowed portals, waiting in vain for his arrival. He'd finally given up the ghost and the holy ghost come to that and passed away to pastures on high to be replaced by the man I like to call 'my vicar'.

It had been while I was waiting for a cup of tea at the social event that I had suddenly found him standing next to me and we had engaged in conversation, some might even call it witty banter. He had remarked about how very fond he was of cakes and scones, especially the home made variety and I had suggested that he might like to come round one afternoon and sample mine. I suppose it had been then that I'd first spotted the twinkle in his eye. I may be sixty but I can still hold my own in the glamour stakes and there is not a lot of competition in that direction in our village, to say the least. When I was subsequently introduced to his wife she struck me as rather a dowdy little thing, pleasant enough but not anyone who would turn a head or elicit a cat call from a building site.

My vicar is in his middle fifties, so I didn't feel as though I was going to be dragging anyone out of his cradle to play with me. He had told me that he was a native of Brixton and how I didn't actually laugh at that, I'm not sure, because it had been obvious that his antecedents had really been natives of somewhere, probably darkest Africa. He is very black, hence the stir when he arrived in the village. I had wondered, as we talked, if he was originally from a Masai tribe who have the reputation of being very tall. He has long arms and legs – well everything about him is long - another reason why he appeals to me.

Anyway, on the following Thursday he had arrived at the front door, promptly at three thirty. I do like a man to be punctual. It says something about him, I always think.

I had laid the little table in the drawing room with all the tea paraphernalia and as it turned out it was over this little table that he first laid me: I had cleared it first you understand. Couldn't damage the best china. Edith would have wanted to know about that and it might have been hard to explain.

Since then Thursday afternoons have been reserved although saying that, there is nothing remotely reserved about them, if you get my drift. I must say I do find them most stimulating and he always goes away with a spring in his step and his appetite satiated, in more ways than one. He's obviously a very spiritual man but he's also incredibly sexy and charming – quite my cup of tea, so to speak. Anyway, we both enjoy our time together.

I took the scones out of the oven and was just thinking that I should go upstairs and change into something more alluring than the shell suit I was wearing when there was a ring at the doorbell.

We weren't expecting anyone to call, especially at 1 o'clock when everyone in the village would be having their lunch. It's no coincidence that the word inhabitant includes the word habit, well in this village it isn't and habit must be strictly adhered to. Anyway, I wiped my hands on the tea towel and headed for the front door.

On opening it I found myself face to face with my vicar's dowdy wife. She stepped over the threshold, uninvited, and hit me full in the face.

"I'll thank you to leave my husband alone, you, you fallen woman!" she snarled, her eyes blazing as I stood there, totally amazed, my nose throbbing as the full force of the blow made itself apparent.

Having looked me up and down a few times, clenching and unclenching her fists by her side and breathing heavily like some bull awaiting its fate in the ring, she turned on her heel and went.

When I said she'd struck me as a very dowdy woman, I had obviously been more prophetic than I had realised.

I retreated to the kitchen and grabbing the tea towel clutched it to my poor nose, now bleeding and possible broken. This was going to go round the village like wild fire.

I looked at the scones, still on their baking tray on the kitchen table. I supposed that Edith and I would have to eat them all ourselves. At that moment, she appeared at the kitchen door. She looked mildly triumphant.

"Oh, dear, whatever is the matter, Martha?" I sensed a trace of irony in her voice. "I thought I heard the bell. Are you hurt dear?" She came across to where I was by now slumped in a chair.

"I saw the vicar's wife leaving from my window." She continued. "Such a nice woman. We do so enjoy our chats at the sewing circle. We talk about simply everything. You ought to join us one day. You might learn something."

I suppose, all things considered, I got away lightly.

Note: The subject we were given was 'bad sex' and this is what I came up with. It is completely fictitious.

MOTHER LOVE

BY CAROLYN SIMS

I knew she was at home before I put the key in the door lock. The house had a tense, wary look about it as if it was waiting for the daily battle that would erupt sometime between five and ten o'clock. Besides, the base beat of some band or whatever was leaking from her bedroom window.

I threw the house and car keys into the basket on the hall table and at the same time shrugged my coat off. There was a straggly mound of mail, advertising leaflets and a few autumn leaves on the door mat. The 'Welcome to Our House' message on the mat did not encourage me to raise my expectations or hopes for a cosy family evening. I struggled into the kitchen carrying the bulging Tesco bag, my school bag, and the assorted mail and dumped the whole lot on the kitchen table. Usually the dog could be relied upon to greet me with his thumping tail, gentle eyes and heavy breathing. Biggles was no intrepid adventurer, unlike his namesake. Any intruder to our home would be greeted warmly with a wagging tail and a hospitable welcome.

"Where are you?" I called "What have I got for you, Biggles?"

I hadn't got anything special for him but he usually responded to the sound of the tin opener and the smell of Pedigree Chum. However, my call remained unanswered so, without the comfort of a dog to stroke and pet, I trudged up the stairs to the base beat coming from Sarah's room.

I tentatively knocked on the door, ignoring the various notices posted on it - 'Private', 'Very Private', 'I want to be alone', 'I'm very busy' and 'Don't even think about it'.

"It's me; Mum." I announced in what I thought was a maternal yet no nonsense tone. The music throbbed through the door as if she had turned the sound up. I thought 'Why do I put up with this?' Why am I subjected to the rudeness and rejection of this girl – this girl who at fourteen can rock my very confidence in myself and my need to love and care for my children? Where is the baby who used to search me out with her eyes, listen to my one sided conversations and explanations as we walked to the shops and the parks? Where is the little girl, thrilled at her role as a lamb in the nursery school nativity play, the bigger girl playing in the recorder band and then, just last year, her clarinet solo in the end of term concert? We used to enjoy each other's company baking and cycling and shopping but now most conversations, if any, are monosyllabic or snarls that would put off a saint.

I knocked at the door again and this time asked if Biggles was with her. A stupid question really because I could hear the thumping of his tail.

"What if he is?" came the reply.

"Well, it's his dinner time. You know how much he expects to be fed at this time."

Silence, well not musical silence as that still thudded gratuitously and monotonously through the walls.

"He can wait tonight, can't he? I need him and he needs me."

"That is unfair, Sarah. You can't use the dog to express your anger," I cautioned.

"Who says I'm angry?"

"Well, I presumed something has happened to make you feel so anxious these past weeks."

"Nothing has happened and I'm not anxious as you so politely put it."

"Sarah, I don't want you to say any more if you are going to be so rude and hurtful. It might be better if you did stay in your room. Please let Biggles out of there so that he can have his dinner. He could come back when he has had his walk. I shall go downstairs to prepare dinner. When you are feeling more sociable we would all love to have you join us."

As I reached the bottom step of the stairs a large missile rocketed past me, tail wagging furiously with pent up pleasure. We carried out our usual mutual greeting of undying love and I had the good sense to call "Thank you" up the stairs. One small victory does not make a battle won but my mood lightened and after feeding the dog and having a quick blitz around the kitchen I was feeling much more optimistic about nothing in particular but hope had not died.

During the next hour the rest of the family returned to the nest.

Number one son, Toby, staggered through the front door, managing to leave it on its hinges but chipping the paint on the frame with his sports bag – was there any sports equipment he did not carry five days a week? Even though I taught at the same school as my children attended I had never quite grasped the complexities of the sports timetable and the equipment it required. But Toby was a healthy and happy twelve year old so who was I to question the value of a love of sport. Maybe that was why Sarah was so fragile and angry. I had read several educational papers that asserted that physical exercise is good for the brain and one's emotional health but who had heard of many teenage girls enjoying PE lessons? I dealt with at least five girls a week who were trying to bunk off from games lessons.

Toby had scattered his possessions from the front door, through the hallway and down to the kitchen like a striptease artiste divesting herself of her underwear. As he reached the biscuit tin he recounted his day at school, the bus ride home and the penalty goal he had scored against a local comp. from Yarmouth and possibly a few more snippets I missed. He ended his diatribe with "What's for dinner? I am starving! Where's grumpy? Do you know her boyfriend's chucked her?"

"How do you know that?" I responded with some interest. "I didn't know she had a boyfriend. Who told you?"

"Oh, everyone knows 'cause he said she didn't love him."

"What? Why did he think that? How long has this been going on for?" I was aware I was firing off questions like gunfire.

"I dunno. Nobody tells me anything."

"Well, you do know this. Why did he think she didn't love him?"

Toby suddenly became quite guarded and he refused to meet my eye as he reached for the biscuit tin again. Before, he had been all gossipy but now he seemed to regret his verbosity.

"Toby, tell me please. She is so unhappy. There must be something I, we, can do".

Toby realised he had dropped the ball, so to speak. He grabbed another biscuit and through a mouthful of crumbs he gabbled "She won't do it – he wanted her to get naked on a selfie."

"What!" I shrieked. All my counselling training was forgotten. This was my daughter dragged into the mire of the twenty first century by some dirty minded, pimply youth. I struggled to contain my agony, anger and fear for my beloved girl. Desperate to know the rest but terrified at the same time, I asked "What happened?"

"He must have told his mates and it's got out,. You know what they're like. Those girls in her year are like vultures. They like to have someone to go for."

I sat down feeling for the chair with one hand and the table with the other. My legs had lost their will to support me and my hands were trembling so badly I could see them leaping around my lap.

"Are you alright Mum? I didn't really want to tell you but everyone knows."

"Thank you darling. You did the right thing. I needed to know."

I pulled myself together and dragged my prematurely ageing body up the stairs to Sarah's room. Biggles seemed to sense his support was required and joined me, his tail thumping encouragingly against my legs.

I knocked on the door and said "Sarah, I know all about it. You're my hero and inspiration. I'm so proud of you. You did the right thing. What a looser he is. If he loved you he wouldn't have asked you to do such a thing. Why would he think a lovely, gifted and beautiful girl like you would want to play such a silly, dangerous and immature game?"

I paused; I desperately did not want to cry.

After a few minutes the monotonous throb was turned off. Biggles pawed at the door and gave an encouraging woof or two. The door opened and my wreck of a daughter stood in the door opening just enough for me to see her tear stained face and the agony written across it. Biggles pushed his way between us. He knew the comfort he could give with his whip lashing tail and fussing around our legs as we held one another.

Later that evening we heard the whole unsavoury story. As my husband, Keith, said, you read about these things but you never think your kids will get involved. We decided, with Sarah's agreement, that Keith would contact 'the boyfriend's' parents on a man to man basis and, as Sarah had not co-operated with the 'photo show', we had no case to present to the school or the police.

We emphasised to Sarah our admiration for her strength of character and tried to offer our support for her against the 'vultures' as Toby had so succinctly described them.

They would look for fresh meat after a few days.

THE LITTLE THERAPY COUNSELLOR

BY HILARY COOMBES

The plummet in Diana's affection began with an aversion to Peter's self-satisfied laugh. Why she had not noticed this earlier in their relationship was a mystery to her. Twelve months into her idyll of rapturous sex she had tired of him. In her entire life she'd never actually been in love with anyone but, at least, Peter had been amusing … for a while.

She thought back to her working life when she first met Peter. He had called her his 'little therapy counsellor'. She was good for him, he'd said.

She felt quite proud when, on their second meeting, he told her she was the only person who understood his mental health difficulties.

The next time they met he'd showed his appreciation with a bunch of flowers that he'd persuaded one of the nurses at the hospital to buy on his behalf.

Peter told her that all of his adult life he had lived with feelings of crippling depression, interspersed with manic bouts of feeling invincible. The invincible Peter had excited her for the hectic, manic mood banished all traces of depression. He was fun to be with then.

It was when his bipolar disorder had finally been diagnosed and his mood swings stabilised with drugs that the seed of possible marriage entered Diana's head. After all she would be in the perfect position to control his moods: plus she had no need to be taught the triggers or signs that a manic episode was about to erupt.

The closure of the psychiatric hospital forced all the patients to move to care in the community. Her first husband's money was running out, so she considered that care in her community might help them both.

They were married within two months of the hospital closure. By this time, Peter was firmly ensconced in her flat and in her bed, and it was the latter that pleased her the most, for she had an insatiable appetite for sex and Peter was good at it. He was especially good when bordering on the manic. She carefully monitored the quantity of mood stabilizers he took to give her the pleasure she sought. She knew this was a dangerous game, but she felt in charge of the situation.

In the early weeks of their marriage, Diana tried to ignore his strange ways. His interfering insistence on the preciseness of food preparation especially annoyed her, but in those early days her mind had been clouded with the rainbow colours produced in the bedroom. With time, the words and actions he used to make her moan in bed were no longer enough.

Peter had disappointed her. This was the man whom she believed would mould to her ways, but no, this was not to be the case. Day by day her irritation with him increased, until she found him as infuriating as her first husband had been.

The day he pinned his homemade poster to the bedroom wall was when she decided it was time to leave him. He'd drawn a crude picture of a naked woman with blood-spattered knives piercing her nipples; the blood from the lacerations ran into the genital area.

In elaborate, blood-red ink underneath he'd written 'Beware Diana. It's sex or death.' She shuddered and made plans to leave next day when Peter would be at the day centre, but had she known what was to happen that night she would have left immediately.

That evening, Diana pleaded tiredness and retired to bed early, planning to be asleep before Peter crawled into bed in the early hours. The plan went badly wrong.

Her sleep was abruptly ended when a terrible sound, like a dog with his leg trapped in barbed wire, pierced her eardrums. Struggling to lose the brain fog of slumber, she heard Peter's voice.

"Hello, my little, slut wife! Surely you're not going to pretend to be asleep, are you? You'll miss all the fun."

He shook her roughly by the shoulders. "Come on! Come on! Time to play with daddy!"

As her eyes adjusted to the gloom of the dimmed light, she could make out Peter's silhouette. He was wearing nothing but his motorbike helmet, and in his hand he brandished a chainsaw that filled the room with its menacing buzz.

Her shrill scream was met by his raucous laughter. In terror she moved to escape, but he was quick and painfully gripped her wrist.

His crazed look terrified her. He threw the live chainsaw noisily across the room. "Where are you going, little wife?" he yelled, as he pushed her flat on the bed and straddled her body. "I thought we were going to have fun."

As he pulled her close she could smell the alcohol on this breath. "You need me, little lady. I'm your man, I'm your Peter, and you, my dear, are my little whore!"

He placed his icy hands around her neck and, as her deprived brain pleaded for oxygen, her senses rapidly shut down. Her heart thudded in her chest and blood pounded in her ears until her hearing was no longer capable of functioning. Her last conscious memory was of shooting bright arrows through a black void, and then she was nothing but a limp, inert body squashed under the weight of a crazed man.

Peter sat on his wife for some time and began singing nursery rhymes, before eventually he clambered off the bed and retrieved the chainsaw that had ricocheted across the floor and come to a halt against the wall.

"See you in the morning, my little therapy counsellor" he snorted as he made his way to the landing, but his little therapy counsellor was no longer in a place where she could hear him. In fact, whether she would be alive in the morning to see him would be a more crucial question.

Next morning the physical sensation of severe pain arrived first, quickly followed by recollection of the previous night. Terror filled Diana's body. Peter was not in bed and, as she struggled painfully to a sitting position, she noticed splattered blood spots on the sheets. Hers or his? She had no idea.

Her anxiety turned to terror when Peter opened the bedroom door. "Oh my love, I am so sorry. Who did this to you? Tell me. I'll kill him. I love you, my little counsellor. I love you."

She flinched as he walked towards the bed.

"No, no, it's your Peter. I won't hurt you. I'm here to look after you."

She stared at him, trying to swallow, but the effort only intensified the pain in her neck. She winced, knowing that the ear pain must also be related. Standing shakily her vision became blurred.

Peter took her hand and gently helped her to sit back on the bed. "I love you! I love you! I love you!" he bellowed which caused her head to join in the pain circus. Kissing her hand over and over, he vowed to take care of her forever. Diana knew that forever was going to be very short … it was too late! He terrified her!

Escape in her present condition would be futile, so she had no choice but to play a waiting game. In his present mood of compassion she hoped Peter might be less of a threat, so playing on her injuries and faking sleep became her way to cope over the next few days.

Peter seemed pleased when she suggested a spa night away with her friend. "Do you good, help you snap out of it!" he brusquely said when she carefully raised the plan. The celibate state of the past few days had to come to an end quickly, he had reasoned, and if this is what would do it, then so be it.

'Shopping therapy' her friend Jill had called the planned night away, but Diana had another more accurate description … 'grief therapy preparation'. She had practised the act of being a grieving widow back in Australia and knew how boring it would be. So a little light therapy beforehand was, she thought, well deserved.

Of course, she made sure that the lithium overdose would be fatal; the first-degree heart block was quickly followed by kidney failure. The cold body she discovered on returning to her flat told her that death probably happened on the Saturday, probably when she was enjoying a meal with Jill hundreds of miles away. She'd purposely asked Jill in for coffee on their return home; an added witness statement she knew was always good.

In the end, ridding herself of Peter had been all too easy, especially when she compared it to the problems involved with the demise of her first husband. At the time there had been an article in the local Sydney paper that she had found uncomfortable; 'mysterious circumstances' it had said, but the coroner made the right decision. Thank goodness!

Of course, she'd made sure there could be no traceable link between her present name and the one she'd used in Australia. All her life she had found it easy to deceive people. They saw a smartly dressed, well-spoken woman, and fell under her spell of deceit. Although even she had been amazed by how easy it had been gaining the hospital job as a Therapy Counsellor. The interviewer had merely glanced over her false Australian qualification papers, and nodded with approval as she told him of her fictitious counselling training and client contact hours.

Living the 'grieving widow' life nine months on had, as expected, been very boring and she was concerned that her second murder was taking longer to fade from her memory than the first one. 'The past is the past' she murmured aloud as she reached for the whisky bottle, 'I have no wish to rejuvenate it', but it was too late. Those past events had woken up the hippocampus of her brain and were going nowhere fast.

When she met John, her now intended third husband, she decided he would never live up to Peter's prowess in bed, but then what did it matter? She felt sure that at least he'd never try to strangle her. He was rich, fun to be with, and said he loved her. In any case she didn't intend that he'd be around long enough to mess up her life.

Listening in the dark to the clock strike two, Diana forced herself to get up. There was no point in lying there listening to the mechanical tick whilst waiting for the illusive blanket of sleep to cover her eyes. It reminded her of her own days incarcerated in the Australian asylum, but even then it had been easy to press the right buttons and manipulate the staff around her. She soon had them believing that the antipsychotic drugs they administered were having a good effect. They'd even given her a privileged free access job in the library. She could have easily escaped then, but that black dog, ever on her shoulder, told her to wait until she was officially free. That way she could disappear without trace.

Pictures of Peter's psychiatric hospital floated around her mind. Its Victorian buildings had been considered archaic long before Diana had first seen them. Locked corridors connected the large, barrack-like rooms where patients lived.

Diana loathed the filthy state of those barrack rooms, and the memory of the urine and faeces-stained toilets were enough to make her shudder. If the imagined smell of patient bodily fluids, ever present on the hoist chairs, managed to invade her consciousness, she knew that within seconds bile would raise in her throat.

How would the therapy counsellor within her treat these sleepless nights and bad memories, she wondered? No, she decided, that would be a slippery road to venture down. After all, an amateur therapy-counsellor who advises herself undoubtedly has a fool for a client.

She poured herself another whisky and endeavoured to force her mind on husband number three.

When her husband-to-be had the audacity to question her on the death of her husband, she hid behind a veil of tears. That he only knew of one death had been a bonus.

Their marriage took place in an elegant, Georgian mansion house situated in its own beautiful grounds near Hampstead Heath, London. John invited a few of his senior staff from work. She had claimed that all her family and friends were in Australia and it was too expensive for them to travel. She had told John that he'd meet them the following year when they took their delayed honeymoon in her home country. Even as she spoke she knew that he'd never leave English soil again.

The smile on her face that wedding day announced Diana's happiness, but not for the reason anyone thought. She had already planned her escape to Thailand as soon as she was a grieving widow once again. She had also decided upon the new name of Caroline Hedges, a nice change from being Diana Foster, she'd thought.

When her wedding night met the morning sun, Diana knew that she might not be able to put up with John for as long as she'd originally planned. She'd sexually kept him at arm's length leading up to their marriage, after all, she had no wish to lose him before the knot was tied, but she hadn't expected such a hopeless, ham-fisted lover in her bed. This was not to her liking at all.

She knew very little about John really. An architect, he'd said, owning his own business. He was certainly well-heeled; his Savile Row suits announced that, plus his large house, which must have been worth a fortune. His Achilles heel was his love of alcohol, something that Diana thought could be a very handy means of escape for her.

She'd researched the symptoms of acute alcohol poisoning, and within a month was well versed with the harm that the traditional ways of sobering someone up could do.

Oh yes, she knew all right, as she carefully planned her method of attack. The next time he rolled home half drunk and continued his alcoholic party at home would be his last. Of course she'd be the perfect wife, give him coffee, make him sick, keep him on his feet, ply him with yet more strong spirits and then let him sleep it off. She'd planned to be alert in the middle of the night and the next morning to continue her nursing role.

Planning this event had sparked an idea. When she was settled in Thailand she would swop the therapy counsellor role for that of a nurse. It seemed an attractive proposition the more she thought about it, and one that would give her ample opportunity to snare husband number four.

'I'll be late tonight, Diana,' John had said as his chauffeur-driven car pulled up on the drive. 'Meetings after work and all that'.

Her mind raced as she stood on the doorstep in her negligee waving him goodbye. So, it was to be tonight; it was a pity that she'd woken up feeling so groggy, a little too much whisky she decided. Still it would probably wear off as the day went on, but for now, she thought, perhaps she'd just grab another hour in bed.

Sunshine had filled the room when she next woke - well, this is probably the wrong description - when she attempted to open her eyes would be more accurate. Squinting with unfocused eyes was the least of her problems, for her heart felt as though it was about to jump out of her body at any minute, and her stomach lurched with the urge to vomit. In fact, she would have been hard-pressed to describe any part of her body that felt normal: pain had invaded even her fingernails. Frothy saliva trickled down her chin as she desperately tried to remember who she was and why she was in this strange room.

It was another hour before she emerged again from her semi-conscious state. Her head now felt as though it would explode and her laboured breathing noisily filled the room, although she was unaware of this.

She was also unaware of the smell of rotten eggs and faeces that surrounded her. It would have been pointless to tell her because her brain was no longer capable of sensible conversation.

Diana never woke again. In fact, when John arrived home, four days later, from the business course that he and his colleagues had attended, the smell had drifted from the bedroom to the hallway. The two men followed the appalling smell to the bedroom and both gasped and, at the same time, gagged when John opened the bedroom door.

Being a shrewd and closet serial killer, John had made sure that another person would accompany him that summer afternoon. He knew that the aconite poison he'd put in Diana's bedtime drink before he'd left home would, by now, have rendered her body stone cold. He also knew that after such a period of time no trace of the poison would be found in Diana's body.

Of course, Diana never did get to Thailand; she had to make do with three husbands. She had met her match with the third who killed simply, for the joy of it and for the thrill of getting away with it, which with Diana's demise he had once again accomplished.

Note: I like to set myself writing challenges, so I will often set out to write in a genre not normally within my writing comfort zone. 'Same-old, same old' can get a bit boring for the reader I think. I wanted to create characters that although the reader could have sympathy for, they would be hard pressed to love them. I also thought a little murder and mayhem might be fun to write. Hope you felt I achieved this and, more importantly, that you enjoyed reading it.

THE VAMPIRE CAT

BY VONNIE GILES

Melek, a rather stunted and strange individual, was skulking behind a newspaper stand at Heathrow Airport. He was waiting for his flight to Transylvania where the VAC (acronym for the Vampire Annual Convention) was going to be held. From his hiding place he could just about see the departure board and could keep up with any changes that might occur. He hoped that there would be no delays, for he wanted a front row seat at the convention, but no one was allowed to book their place beforehand – it was all on a first-come, first-served basis. Last year he had ended up sitting on a window sill right at the back of the hall, without even the comfort of a cushion as compensation. With so many privately chartered flights from all over the world converging on Transylvania on the same day, he mustn't get his hopes set too high.

Right now he was dressed in the disguise that he usually wore when appearing in a public place: the sort of tight, woollen skull cap favoured by skiers which hid his furry pointed ears; a mask that he hoped would make people think that he was merely the victim of some horrible accident; gloves to cover his claws; his body swathed in a black robe reminiscent of a high church prelate, without the crucifix, of course, because he wasn't quite sure that he believed in all that.

His whiskers, however, were the main problem because he couldn't judge distances if they were covered. Consequently he'd almost pushed over the newspaper stand in his rush to join the queue when his flight was announced.

He obediently placed his small piece of hand luggage under the seat in front of him and stowed his packet of fish and blood sandwiches in the seat pocket. The stewardess, seeing that he would have problems, was kind enough to fasten his seat belt. His final thought was to make sure that his passport was still safely tucked in his robe pocket with all its correct information. His name: Melek V. Cat. His address: a squat somewhere in Gloucestershire. His next of kin in case of an emergency: Miss Ariadne Ponsonby.

Once he was settled, he looked around to see if there was anyone that he recognised among his fellow passengers. Sure enough, there was Ron Vampire sitting further down from him. Ron was an important leader of the feline section of the brotherhood and had more victims to his name than anyone else. Horrendously brutal, with a snarl to outmatch that of any alpha male in the jungle, his heavily tattooed and pierced body that had been partly shaved to show everything to its best advantage, was hidden by a stylish Burberry coat. In superb physical condition with fangs sharpened to the finest point, he was a worthy successor to Dracula. Melek tried to put Ron's tattoos out of his mind as did most of the other vampires: not a pretty sight and certainly not the subject to contemplate before eating one's sandwiches.

Melek was terribly excited to be travelling on the same flight as Ron – what a start to the journey! He just hoped that he would be noticed by him – perhaps as he waddled down to the loo he might stop and have a few words with Ron. He didn't think that this would be too much of a presumption; after all it was the civil thing to do and Melek did like to think of himself as a true gentleman.

Soon his sandwiches had been satisfyingly consumed together, unfortunately, with a couple of Bloody Marys, which is where the trouble started. The consumption of alcohol was not something that Melek regularly indulged in, but having seen Ron, he'd become somewhat hyped-up and daring, so that when he finally tottered off to the loo he was none too steady on his back legs and there was a definite mist in front of his eyes, his ears ringing. His front paws were rather wobbly too; hence, although he'd used a straw, the splatter of tomato juice all over his mask reminded his fellow passengers of someone who had just been drinking blood.

It so happened that on this particular flight only a minority were headed for the convention; the majority being members of a Welsh male choir on a European tour. Using the arms of the aisle seats to steady himself, he finally found himself approaching Ron, but failed to notice that Ron's feet were sticking out. He fell over them and the next thing he heard was a deafening roar and found himself moving at a great speed down the aisle on top of the food trolley on to which he had been flung.

Ron had risen from his seat and was doing his diva act, making no end of a commotion so that all the passengers thought that this was some sort of theatrical turn that Transylvania Airlines had put on for their entertainment. Melek and Ron received a terrific round of applause for their performance. Nevertheless, two plain-clothes security guards sitting in the back row realised that this was something out of the ordinary and quickly handcuffed both of them, although it was touch and go as to whether they could actually contain Ron. Melek had flexed his claws in a knee-jerk reaction to this assault, and had accidently drawn blood from a woman passenger's arm which was rather appropriate considering their destination. She spent the rest of the journey happily wondering whom she could sue and how much recompense she might receive for her injury. Taking plenty of selfies, she hoped that the small scratch would continue to bleed as much as possible until they reached Transylvania. However, no one was going to Transylvania that day, for the pilot sensibly decided to return to London.

Melek pulled off his mask and opened his mouth so wide that everyone could see exactly what he was; his fangs covered in tomato juice protruded in a very off-putting way from a crescent-moon opening that stretched from ear to ear: Cheshire-cat-style, but more extreme. He'd also got roast beef, mashed potatoes and gravy all over his black robe at which he started to lick as though he were starving.

So back to Heathrow they all went. Down on the tarmac two police car were waiting and, heavily guarded, the two miscreants descended to await their fate: Ron Vampire and a tabby cat who thought he was a vampire and thus had ideas far above his station. As they went down the steps they could hear the male voice choir giving them a resounding send-off with "All Through the Night" sung at full volume.

Melek, however, had had a lucky escape for none of this nonsense was his true life: merely one of those visions of the impossible in which his vivid imagination sometimes indulged.

It was a beautiful English summer day, a dreamy Cotswolds day as the sun beamed down with a smile on its face upon the picture-postcard cottages and churches. Miss Ariadne Ponsonby, tall and stately, stood by the open sitting-room window watching Sid sleeping on the window sill. He was a darling tabby cat and she was so glad that she had given him a home. He'd been found abandoned, left to his own devices, in a squat in Gloucester where apparently the down-and-outs had given him the very grand name of Melek, but she just called him Sid.

Sid was stretched out, luxuriating in the warmth. Opening his eyes, he was rather surprised and very relieved not to see the police waiting for him as he left the Transylvania Airlines' plane. The only things to meet his eyes were hollyhocks, lupins and sunflowers; the only sounds those of bees buzzing and of Miss Ponsonby singing a little tune to herself. His sole regret was his name. Surely a cat of his calibre deserved something better, something more imaginative, than Sid.

SWALLOWED WHOLE

BY OWEN SUTHERLAND

A mutineer avoiding familiar chores

I flee to distant foreign shores

But the spirits stir the ocean's loins

Snorting waves snatch at the vessel's hull

I am sacrificed to soothe this tempest angry beast

And so my drowning body is cast adrift.

I lie panting on a shingle beach

A trembling tongue among the flailing waves

A harbour haven from my nightmare seas

A sanctuary for souls who've lost their minds

Imagined safety from the seasick fear

A refuge from reality water on the brain.

Now the sky like the heavy lid of a sarcophagus

Presses me down into the coffin of stone walls

Embalming me in drenching drowning acid rain

Stripping my flesh etching my bones with aching pain

The only escape the gaping mouth of the cathedral

Belching its sweet sickly breath its siren call of safety.

Inside the cold quiet of death clings to the walls

And shivers into my sodden clothes steeps me in awe

Now in the silence I hear the chanting of the organ

Feel eddies of spirits flowing in the darkness

And travelling deeper through the entrails of the creature

Emerge into a vast cavern – a lantern of light.

Tall columns of white shrinking into the infinity of height

The skeleton of some mammoth beast with chiselled teeth

Passing through the congregation of pawns at prayer

To cloistered coils of winding ways

Where the boxed bones of former habits rest

Their souls released from the ribbed cells of their mortal test.

So many shrimps sieved from the seas

Food for the leviathan crushed to conformity

Lives spent as krill to a selfish deity

Their skeletons laid down to build this divinity

The monstrous obscenity to man's hubris

A supernatural construction shark of the Holy See.

A harpoon hidden in the soft tissue of towering flesh

A spluttering candle in the chandelier of my head

A whine of winches dragging me from death

A reek of burning blubber wrenches me awake

Swearing whalers hacking stone and laying it to rest

A cathedral of curses submerging in the depths.

The sun rising over the silent sea

Fresh air inside me as my nostrils clear

Life goes on outside the sinking ship of fear

I'm reborn a dolphin out of school

Free to roam and wonder with no imagined rules

Friends with shrimp and lobster a member of the crew.

Note: Our writing topic was "A wet weekend in Whitby". The topic brought whaling to mind then, on visiting Burgos Cathedral, the comparison of its enormity and structure to that of a whale seemed worth pursuing. The images of a wet and wild storm, old square rigged whaling ships, religion and sacrifice led to the story of Jonah. We cannot escape from being human – with all the pressures that brings – we can only dream of freedom.

DAISY'S DIARY

BY MADDY PATTERN

Friday 13th April 1979

It's 10.30 pm and having slept on & off for most of the evening, am now tucked up in bed with an Ovaltine and two more paracetamol. I have decided to start writing a diary in the beautiful red leather bound notebook that my Dad gave me years ago and which has been gathering dust in my bookcase. So before I nod off, am going to start putting down thoughts and daily happenings in my life.

Today was Friday 13th and, true to superstition, it was a pretty bloody awful day! I have felt a little unwell for a couple of days, achy with a pounding headache. Took two paracetamol, then hopped into the shower...swore out loud...no effing hot water! It wasn't the first time and I needed to face the fact I would have to buy a new boiler. It's 15 years old now and, like a few other things in my flat, which Dad had bought in 1964 just off Oxford Street, it is falling apart, as I appear to be! After wrapping a large towel round myself I noticed some rather odd spots on my chest! Really? I'm 35 years old for Gods sake; I finished with spots in my late teens! Was supposed to be going out with Tim tonight as well!

I went off to work feeling like I had done a round with Muhammad Ali. I've been working as a librarian in the historical section of the London Library for the past 15 years, and was lucky to have secured the position when I left the comprehensive in Birmingham with a few exams. Today, though, I thought I caught several people staring at me! Well, I know I'm no oil painting, pretty mousy looking really, and my green eyes probably being my only redeeming feature! Lunchtime I went off to the ladies to see if perhaps I had grown horns or my hair was standing on end like one of the Sex Pistols! No...it was worse than that! More spots had appeared above my shirt collar on my neck and a couple stood out on my chin! Went to speak to my supervisor, Miss Lemon, who lives up to her name, as she always looks as though she's been sucking one!! Anyway, she just stared at me, grimaced, put her hand to her mouth, moved back several paces and sent me straight home!

By 3.30 pm, I discovered more blotchy spots, my glands were up and I was aching all over! Took two more paracetamol and thought of my Dad, wishing he were still around, knowing he would have looked after me. It would have been useless ringing my mum as she would put the phone down immediately! She and my brother had never got over the fact that Dad had left me all his money! No surprises there...mum had poured vodka down her throat whilst Mick snorted white powder up his nose! My poor Dad; he had left them and taken me with him. We had lived here happily until my brother had attacked him in the street with a carving knife, wanting money! Dad had died in hospital and Mick is now serving out a life sentence in Pentonville prison! Bastard, hope he rots in hell! The whole thing had left me feeling angry, bereft and abandoned! A feeling which still overwhelms me on occasion!

I rang Tim and called off our date, explaining that I was covered with weird spots! He just grunted and mumbled something about chicken! It was a bad line and I wondered why he was babbling on about chicken! Stupid man! I then plonked myself on the sofa and switched on the TV...tennis! Well, anything that took my mind off the spots which are starting to itch, plus Tim's idiotic, brief conversation! I was actually relieved not to be seeing him and had started thinking about finishing the relationship, which really was going nowhere! To be honest having him in my bed was beginning to make me feel slightly queasy! He has the most repulsive feet I've ever seen on anybody! Nail fungus, skin falling off the soles of his feet and they smell worse than the camembert cheese in my fridge!

The tennis on the TV was pretty boring and I found myself thinking and dreaming of being the supervisor of the history section in the Library and Miss Sourpuss having been sacked for using appalling language to a customer! At that point I must have nodded off, waking every now and then before finally going to bed and writing down about my awful day!

Saturday 14th April 1979

Am very unwell! Have spots everywhere now! I look like Mount Vesuvius erupting! Rang the surgery describing my condition and how ill I felt, and asked for a home visit. The receptionist told me the doctor would call in at lunchtime after his morning surgery.

Well, the doctor came! Apparently, I have Chicken Pox and have to stay home until the spots scab over and try not to scratch! Oh joy! So that's what Tim was on about. Maybe, he's not so stupid after all! But I really cannot put up with his feet anymore!

Friday 27th April 1979

Having not picked up a pen for a couple of weeks to write anything down here, I have promised myself, again, that I will do it every evening in bed.

Well, I've recovered from my chicken pox, thank God! Have been very unwell, but luckily no scars on my face, just one or two on my arms, and in my left groin! Yes, I had spots everywhere, even down there! You can imagine trying to put calamine lotion through a mountain of hair...It looked as though my pubes had gone white overnight!!

Still, that's over with. Obviously haven't been at work, but return on Monday. Wonderful! My supervisor, Miss Lemon, in fairness, had been fairly understanding and, judging by her phone calls to me, insisted I didn't return until the spots had gone!

As for Tim? Well, I tried to give him the heave ho, but he obviously didn't get the gist of what I was telling him, because he turned up out of the blue on the day after the doctor had been and diagnosed chicken pox. He apparently had had it! I couldn't really refuse him as he said he'd bought some more calamine lotion for me and a Chinese take-away for us both! But when I let him in, the smell turned my stomach and I had to rush to the loo where I was violently sick! I then told him he had to eat it in the bathroom when I had finished there. Which he did, fair play to him! He then came over most days with bits and pieces and I didn't have the heart or feel well enough to tell him we were finished! Luckily, my illness has put him off anything to do with the bedroom, so haven't had to endure his smelly feet!

After a week or so, and I didn't know whether to laugh or cry, not over my incredibly itchy body, but the fact that Tim had come down with it too! His phone call to tell me he'd caught it and that he felt awful made me snigger! I'd had to pretend I was sneezing! So much for him having had it before! Apparently, his sister was looking after him...well, I couldn't, could I? When he's better I will have to tell him that I cannot see him anymore and that we really aren't suited. Gulp...Don't want to hurt him, but, apart from his appalling feet, we really have nothing in common.

Saturday 28th April 1979

Woke up feeling the joys of spring and decided to do just that and have a complete spring clean of the flat. It needed it...as I hadn't done any housework since I became ill.

Had a lovely cooked breakfast and went down to check my post box. A couple of letters and a rather formal looking envelope with HMP on the front!

In trepidation, I opened it, only to find a letter informing me that my brother, who had stabbed my father to death some 14 years ago wanting money to feed his drug habit, had been granted parole and had given my address as the one he would be staying at on his release! Was this okay? What the hell! No bloody way!! I whipped out my writing pad and envelopes and wrote a furious letter back, saying that there was no chance whatsoever that he was going to be living with me now, or at any time in the future!

I put the spring cleaning to one side; that could bloody wait! This was far more important. I whizzed down to the Post Box to post it. I felt quite sick, very sick. The bastard could find somewhere else to live...and why not at his mother's? They could kill themselves slowly together. Her with the booze and him with the drugs. No I wasn't having any of it.

Sunday 29th April 1979

Have spent the day feeling like shit and watching equally mindless shit on the telly!

Monday 30th April 1979

Woke up feeling anxious and fearful. Back to work as well. Got dressed in my grey working suit and white blouse, had breakfast and went off to catch the bus to work. It seemed strange to be going back after nearly 3 weeks.

Arrived and went to the Ladies to leave my coat. A couple of other women were in there yabbering away, but stopped in mid flow when they saw me. Oh crap, I thought, what now? One of the women, April, asked how I was and then giggled! I stood there for a minute of two, said I was much better and what was going on? Nothing, nothing, they replied in unison! Shaking my head, I left my coat on a hanger and went off to my domain in the history section and Miss Lemon!

Strange, there was no Miss Lemon in sight! I started to clear the piles of read books on the trolley when someone tapped me on my shoulder. Startled, I turned and there was Mr. Booker, yeah, yeah, that really is his name. He's one of the directors of the library. Smiling at me, he put both hands on my shoulders! Yikes, no...he had a reputation for being a bit of a ladies man, so tried to move back. He wasn't going to add me to the list of his conquests from the library! As the saying goes, I was fed up not hard up! Anyway, he got the hint and stood back still beaming at me, clasping his hands together in front of him. Bemused, I realised his mouth was moving and was congratulating me on my promotion! Promotion? Unbelievably, it seemed that I had been promoted to Supervisor of the history section and that my wages would rise too. To be honest I was gobsmacked. I then asked him what had happened to Miss Lemon? He told me that the week before, poor Miss Lemon had been sucking one of her favourite sweets, Sherbet Lemons...Yes, I know, how ironic...when she had accidently swallowed it whole, whilst trying to suck the sherbet out of the end, and ended up choking to death...despite the ambulance men who had tried to revive her. I murmured shocked responses, well I was shocked, anyone would be, wouldn't they? However, I am now the supervisor...Yippee! No more sour comments from Miss Lemon. I am the boss! In darkness there is light! I fairly skipped to my new office, delegating dear April to sorting out the books on the trolley. What pleasure that gave me!

The day passed wonderfully in my new role. Things, at last, were looking up!

THE GIFTS OF CHANCE

BY ROBERT WEBB

Tokyo, Japan - 9am, Saturday, April 18th 1942.

It was a fine, spring day, without a cloud in the blue Tokyo sky.

Delicate pink cherry blossom was everywhere to be seen in the city's open spaces, and the neighbourhood where Tomoji and Kikuno Sato lived was quiet for a Saturday.

The taxi they had ordered arrived on time to take their daughter Michiko to Tokyo railway station in the Chiyoda district. From there, she would travel by train the fifty-five kilometres to Hiratsuka City, and then be taken to the accommodation provided for female workers. On Monday she would begin her job on the production line for war munitions, as instructed by the Japanese Minister of Munitions, Nobusuke Kishi.

Michiko had volunteered for this new government programme which was to enlist female labour and boost the war effort. She would be living with many other young women in the specially-built quarters near the factory. In the past, Japanese women had not been permitted to work in manufacturing, but the beginning of war with America a few months before had created the need for a rapid rise in the production of armaments. Japan needed many more machines of war, and the weapons, ammunition and bombs which went with them.

As she left the house, Michiko put down her small case and turned to her parents, placed her hands together as if praying, and then bowed from the waist, as was the usual custom. Unlike westerners, even close family members in Japan did not hug or kiss each other.

"Goodbye, dearest Father and Mother", she said, with a tremor in her soft voice, "I shall think of you every day".

Both parents bowed in return, and Michiko's mother could not prevent herself from shedding a tear as she did so. Their daughter was just nineteen years old and about to live away from the family home for the first time.

"We shall miss you very much, dear Musume-san. Please write soon and let us know that you are doing well in your new job. If you need anything you must tell us", said Kikuno.

She turned to her husband for his nod of agreement, and saw that Tomoji had also just wiped a tear from his own eye.

Michiko got into the taxi, they each waved their goodbyes, and the car drove away.

To deal with their feelings of emptiness in the house now that Michiko had gone, the couple decided to busy themselves by tending their small garden. It needed some work to restore its well-ordered symmetry after a week of winds and rain showers.

Later, just before midday, they stopped for some tea in the sunshine. Their peaceful morning was interrupted, though, by the increasingly loud noise of heavy aircraft engines and they both looked up to the sky to see the source of the disturbance. Years of war and conflict with the Chinese and Russians meant that they had seen and heard many things, but this was not an engine sound they recognised.

Then, there was a loud burst of fire from an anti-aircraft gun, three huge explosions and an earth-shattering thud nearby. It was obviously not just a Japanese Air Force flying exercise.

"Surely not the Chinese?!" Tomoji said to his wife, as they both got up to run for shelter.

"It is not important who, dear husband, just as long as -- ". Her reply was lost in the devastating impact of an incendiary bomb exploding a few yards from where she had been standing. Kikuno was killed instantly. In moments, the world had changed from a peaceful garden of happiness to an inferno of burning rubble, smoke and dust.

Tomoji had been a little further from the blast than his wife, and although he hadn't taken the full force of the explosion as she had, nevertheless he was mortally wounded. He fell to the ground, his back broken and with injuries to his head. He knew that very soon he would be joining Kikuno in the next world.

As is often claimed by those who have been close to dying, Tomoji's life seemed to pass before his eyes as he drifted into unconsciousness. The trauma of the explosion had caused his mind to lose its focus on reality for a minute or so. Then, when he had regained some awareness, all he could do was to lie helplessly on the ground, anxious and fearful of what would become of Michiko now she would be without a mother and father in life.

Tomoji did not know what exactly had befallen Tokyo, but at least dear Michiko had been lucky to escape death that day. He forgot his pain for a few moments and wept heavy tears for his beloved wife Kikuno, and the daughter he would now never see again.

Then the stillness of death finally embraced him.

Hiratsuka City, Japan - Monday, 20th April, 1942

The news of her parents' death was eventually received by Michiko from an uncle who lived near her family home in Tokyo.

Japan had been completely surprised and enraged by this Tokyo bombing. Yes, there were many practice air raid drills after years of conflict with China and the continued poor relations with Russia, but despite the start of war with America just a few months before, the Japanese had thought the distance between the two countries was so great that they would surely be safe from any bombing raids by the Americans.

It seemed that the Sato family's great misfortune was to live close to a steel mill targeted by the Americans. Michiko's father had, in fact, been a well-respected salaryman there.

The Tokyo newspapers and radio reported that American heavy bombers had somehow been launched from an aircraft carrier in Pacific waters within range of Japan. It was in revenge for the Japanese attack on Pearl Harbour a few months before. The American bombers had killed many civilians and children in the Tokyo area, as well as in Yokohama and Osaka, after which they had flown beyond the islands of Japan to land in China. There would now be a hunt for the crews of these aircraft in the regions of mainland China that Japan now controlled.

Despite her deep sorrow, Michiko had been given no choice but to begin work at the factory as she had been directed. After these bombings by America, she was told that war work at home was even more urgent. She wanted to leave this place and be alone with the grief she felt for her parents, but where would she go? Her home was no more. She had to accept that the best way to deal with her sadness was to put it aside and concentrate on working hard to help her country defeat its enemies.

As the months turned into years and the war in the Pacific continued, Michiko and the other women at Hiratsuka endured long hours, little pay, poor working conditions and a constant shortage of food. To make matters worse, the men at the factory treated the women as inferiors, despite their hard work and superior skills for many of the tasks required of the job.

Michiko had hoped in vain that the war would end within a year, but it was not to be. The longer it continued, the more she had to motivate herself to be positive about the future. At first, like most of the women, she often liked to dream that when the war was over she might become the loving wife of perhaps a handsome young officer in the Imperial Japanese Navy.

However, this dream was wearing ever thinner and her opinion of men became sullied by the attitude of the male workers around her at the factory. She suffered them in silence every day, but would never forget their callous treatment of the women. She worried that perhaps there would not be any good young men left in Japan when the war finally ended, and when the death toll was counted.

Finally, Michiko decided to stop dreaming of love and marriage as a worthy ambition for the future. It now seemed a pointless exercise that would only end in disappointment and regret. There should be more to life than devoting and subjugating yourself to the needs and demands of a man. In a way, Michiko was almost grateful to the awful male factory workers around her. They had forced her to re-consider what life should be about, and somehow she felt a new freedom within herself.

It was certainly a release of some kind, and while she tried to make sense of it, the feeling helped to sustain her through the difficult and troubling times ahead.

Japanese Navy Arsenal, Kokura, Japan - March, 1944

After two years, and as a result of a steep rise in the number of American bombing raids on Tokyo, Michiko and her fellow female workers were transferred to other armaments facilities thought to be less vulnerable to attack. Michiko herself was sent to the Navy arsenal at Kokura, in the south west of Japan. Once again, she and the other women had to suffer poor work and living conditions, scarce food, and the disrespect of the men around them. It was almost as if Japanese men saw women as their enemies, not as hard-working colleagues and compatriots.

To make matters worse, later that year the Americans began bombing Japan from bases in India and China, and so Kokura itself became more vulnerable as a target. The Americans now also had larger and longer-range bombers than ever before. They flew too high for Japanese anti-aircraft guns to reach them. No longer concentrating just on major cities, the Americans were fire-bombing urban areas where small family workshops and private homes manufactured parts for the Japanese war effort.

Michiko once again remained fortunate not to be one of the many casualties inflicted on the Japanese people during this campaign.

Kokura, Japan - 10.30a.m., 9th August, 1945

One day in August 1945, an American B-29 bomber had orders to fly to Japan and drop its payload on the Kokura arms factory, releasing the deadly explosive only upon a clear, visual identification of the target.

A young American airman looked though his bombsight and could see some of the buildings of Kokura and the river that ran by the arms factory, but the complex itself was blocked by cloud. After the third attempt to sight its target clearly, but with clouds still obscuring the view, the B-29 pilot gave up on Kokura.

It decided to go on to its secondary target, Nagasaki, one hundred and fifty kilometres south west of Kokura.

The plutonium bomb which had been meant for Kokura killed over one hundred thousand people in Nagasaki instead.

EPILOGUE

Kanazawa Retirement Community, Ishikawa Prefecture, Honshu Island, Japan, March, 2012

Michiko Sato enjoyed her ninetieth birthday very much. She was in good health, and all of her friends were at the small party given in her honour by the elderly care community where she now lived.

After dedicating a toast to her, ("Kampai!") the small group who had gathered for the occasion – all women – asked her what she thought were the reasons for her longevity.

"I have been very fortunate. You could say that it has been a charmed life. A life of many lucky escapes. I have always managed to survive by what is sometimes called the gift of chance – and, of course, what I have always believed is my own independent spirit."

Michiko continued, as the women around her remained quiet and almost reverential in their silent attention to her words.

"I have tried to remain independent from what the world of men forces upon us every day and every year. Bloody wars, the chains of religion, daily servitude, great inequality, domestic violence, drunkenness, infidelity, desertion...".

She paused and remained silent for several seconds, not wanting to appear too zealous, or indeed bitter, on the subject.

The room went quiet. Then one of the newer women in the community spoke.

"Have you never loved a man or been married, then, Michiko?"

They all laughed, some more loudly than others.

"Not married," replied Michiko. "...but I have had lovers. I am not a celibate nun, heaven forbid. I thought about marriage many times during my life. But I looked at the world around me that was controlled by men. I considered the lives of every married woman I had known as a friend. Then I weighed all of that against the freedom and independence I had always enjoyed in my life... the freedom to be myself, not what others wanted me to be.... and finally I decided that remaining single had been my luckiest escape of all!"

TEMPTATION

BY JOHN ROSS

He had never done anything like this before, not even thought of it, but here he was in a hotel bar with Sheila, a family friend.

Sheila was in her early forties, a few years older than him, but there was something about her that attracted him like a moth to a flame.

She had always dressed well and tonight was no exception; heels, black dress that seemed to act like a second skin, small, gold chain around her neck, dangling earrings that sparkled as she laughed, lipstick that was dark and red and eyes that were immaculately made up to show off the green of the pupils that dragged men in. She stood just under five feet five in her stockinged soles but, in the heels, she was just slightly shorter than his five feet ten inches.

Pat Andrews was pushing forty. His marriage to Linda was having a few problems, and he had no idea why. He was in his prime; he was a Senior Financial Advisor with Countonit, a private financial advisory company focussing on high wealth customers in the Far East and Middle East, mostly in Hong Kong and Dubai. The role entailed him travelling to these countries to meet clients, as well as using the office in Knox Street in Marylebone, London and Plaza de las Solidaridad, Malaga. He was earning a six-figure sum, their only son had just gone to University in Exeter and Linda had gone back to work as a PA for the M.D. of an Insurance Company in the City.

They both commuted from the four-bedroom, double-garage, detached in Sandelswood End, Beaconsfield, a quiet collection of prestigious houses less than an hour by train from Central London. The area was affluent and the houses expensive - the house seven doors down had sold for £1.2M a few years ago. They had bought their house almost a 12 years ago from the lawyer who was administering the estate of an old lady who had died, and whose family lived in Australia. They had bought it for just over £300,000 and had spent another £100,000 on it. He reckoned it was now worth about £1M more than he paid for it and it was all equity. His car was a Mercedes CLS saloon and she drove another Mercedes, an ML350. They had genuine Rolex watches, and wore designer clothes both for business and for casual. He played Golf at the Beaconsfield Golf Club where annual fees were in excess of £7000.

So why wasn't everything good?

He had arranged to meet Sheila for a chat at the Savill Court Hotel in Englefield Green, far enough away from Beaconsfield for it to be unlikely that they would meet anyone that they would know, but near enough to be just 30 minutes away from Beaconsfield. What was he hoping to achieve? Did he really think that Sheila could help? She had gone through a break up and divorce three years ago and came out the other side well provided for; her husband had not and ended up taking a job in Singapore. He wanted her opinion on where he stood, at least that was what he told himself.

He had arrived at the hotel car park and made his way to the bar, got a lime and soda and made himself comfortable in one of the leather sofas by the large windows.

The bar was a horseshoe extending from one wall facing the length of the room that contained an assortment of tables and chairs, mostly leather and dark wood. The bar staff wore a uniform of white shirt with red tie, striped trousers and black waistcoat. The atmosphere was sophisticated, but impersonal. He checked his smartphone for messages. There was none that needed dealing with and, as he slipped it back into the inside pocket of his grey suit jacket. He looked up and saw her standing there. He stood, and she walked over -welcoming embraces and air kisses over, she sat down, the black dress revealing legs clad in sheer nylon, and he was sure that they were not tights.

"A drink, madam?" asked the waiter.

"Yes, a G&T with a slice."

As the waiter walked off to get the drink, she looked at Pat. His brown hair was still brown, no signs of grey yet, and she liked the way that he wore it just slightly too long, as if it should have been cut two weeks ago. It suited him.

He was fit and carried very little fat, a tribute to the health spa and gym at the golf club and the running that he did when he had time. His tie was a mix of red, grey and gold, Italian she assumed. The cut of the shirt and suit betrayed what it cost and the highly polished Loake shoes finished off the ensemble. He looked like a well-heeled businessman meeting a client.

"So, what can I do for you, Patrick?" She had always used his full name. He found it both irritating and endearing.

He took a sip from his drink, the ice clinking in the glass. "Well, as you know things are not great between Linda and me and haven't been for some time now. We just seem to be becoming distant. We live together, but seem to be on different planets. She went back to work a few months ago and it feels like it all started then. She has new horizons that I can't see. She works long hours and comes home tired. The conversation is pretty much 'how was your day' with monosyllabic answers. I don't know what to do."

The waiter arrived with Sheila's drink: coaster put on the table, glass put on the coaster, another coaster put on the table on to which a small jug of tonic water was carefully placed. The waiter stood erect and smiled, then walked off back to the bar, seemingly happy with what he had done as if he was a magician who had just pulled a dozen pigeons out of thin air.

As Sheila leaned forward to mix her drink, he caught a glimpse down the front of her dress. She did not notice, or did she just choose to ignore it?

"Ah, at last!" She picked up the jug and poured the tonic into the glass and took a large gulp. "That is so much better."

Placing the glass back on the table, she stared straight at him. "Is she screwing around?"

He was so taken aback that he actually recoiled in the sofa. "No. Absolutely not."

The statement started off strong and confident, but there was a hint of question at the end.

"Are you sure?"

"I think so. I mean, she wouldn't do that. We've been together since we met at University."

"So, just over 20 years together and never a doubt?"

The glass was back at those deep red lips, the question hung in the air.

"No, never. Well, I never really thought about it." He was swirling his empty glass around in his hand. The waiter took that as a signal and came over to the table.

"Another, sir?"

"What?" he looked up at the interruption and then down at his glass. "Yes, yes I'll have a G&T, same as the lady."

"And I'll have another," she added.

The waiter turned and walked back towards the bar and they both looked around them. The bar was starting to fill up. It looked like a business conference or training course. There were about twelve men, all in suits and ties with conference badges pinned on their lapels, and about half that number of women in a mixture of trouser suits, skirts and jackets, the conference badges pinned on to their handbag straps as they all milled around the bar placing orders.

"Looks like we have company," Sheila laughed. "Might be a delay in the service."

There was something in the way that she said 'service' that made him smile, then he felt guilty. He shifted in his seat, flicked a non-existent piece of lint from his trouser crease, coughed and looked back at Sheila who was smiling, her eyes sparkling in the fading sun coming through the window.

Was he really here to find answers, or to find something else? His thoughts were interrupted by the waiter returning with the two gin and tonics which he laid on the table with a flourish, followed by a smile and a quick turn on his heels back to the group that was growing larger at the bar. Instinctively they both lifted their glasses and made the universal slight movement of the hand indicating cheers. He looked lost. She looked happy.

"So, if she's not screwing around, are you two still screwing?" The directness stunned him and at the same time gave a frisson to the conversation that excited him. Sheila returned her glass to the coaster, smiled and re-crossed her black nylon clad legs, in what to him seemed a slightly exaggerated and slow fashion, giving him a glimpse up the hem of the dress.

"Well, we are still having sex, not very often though, as we both work long hours and get home tired. You know how it is: commute, work, commute, eat, sleep, repeat." He gulped a too large mouthful of G&T and felt the lump of it as he tried to swallow.

"That's no excuse. A man of your age should be having sex several times a week and making the time for it. When Steven and I were still on good terms we were at it like rabbits, all over the house, in the car, in hotels." Her eyes bored right into Pat. "Even when we were not on such great terms, near the end, before he slunk off to Singapore, we were still at it." Her eyes left his and strayed towards the ornate, plaster coving above the window. "Anyway, if you are not doing it then the rot sets in, the gap widens, and it becomes very difficult to restart. That's when they start looking for pastures new and move on."

Sheila took another sip of her drink; the rim of the glass already held a slight red shade from her lipstick which he couldn't help but look at.

He pulled himself together, "No I don't believe she is looking elsewhere and I know that we are not having sex as regularly as some, but there is more to life than sex. There's companionship, trust, sharing experiences, not having to speak because you know what each other will say."

"Christ! Are you living in a retirement home already, Patrick? Where's the fun, where's the excitement, the spontaneity?" She waved the glass wide with her right hand, "There's a whole world out there," as if she was pointing to it with the gin glass, "and you and Linda are watching it go by, like spectators. You need to go out there and grab it, enjoy it, relish it before it's too late."

Patrick suspected that she had been drinking before she arrived as she was becoming very demonstrative. Thankfully the crowd, some of whom were still around the bar, the rest having grabbed a few tables and put them together, were so wrapped up in themselves that they ignored both of them.

"I know what you mean and to be honest we have done that. We had our heyday before we had Ian. We had weekends away together when he was older. We have had fun."

"'Had', Patrick, 'had'. Isn't that the problem? It's all in the past and coming up for forty you have nothing to look forward to: a wife you barely touch and a son who is in bloody Exeter. What do you want?" She was leaning forward, the glass still in her right hand, her neck extended allowing the earrings to jangle and sparkle as a distraction to him from the view down her dress. "Well, what do you want, Patrick?" she repeated. "Advice from me: I took Steven for every penny I could. You don't want that to happen to you, do you? I have no idea how your finances are structured, but if you are looking to exit a twenty-year-plus marriage with the assets that you have, you need to prove that she is the one at fault otherwise, my poor Patrick, you will lose and lose badly. Where's that bloody waiter? I could do with another drink."

Her head turned towards the bar and the waiter bobbed his head slightly. She had that effect on people.

"I don't know what I am looking for, and I certainly don't know what Linda is looking for."

"First off, ask yourself and be honest, make a sodding list of what you want, then sit Linda down and do the same. Get her to be honest, compare the list and take it from there. If that doesn't work, then try counselling, assuming you both still want to stay together." The waiter appeared with another large G&T for Sheila, placed it on the table, removed the empty glasses and looked at Pat. "Anything else, sir?"

"No, not for me, not at the moment."

"Very good, sir." He smiled, turned on his heel and retreated to the bar.

"Look, Patrick, you are a good-looking man, you've done well, you deserve a bit of fun in your life and if Linda isn't it, then you need to look elsewhere." She sat up straight in the leather chair and smiled at him, as she took a long, slow sip from the fresh glass. The green eyes over the rim of the glass were drawing him in like a magnet. "And you don't have to look very far, you know." The glass was returned to the table, her arms lay on the leather of the well-upholstered chair, the legs were uncrossed and crossed again, the meaning was obvious.

He was caught in a quandary. He had been looking to save his marriage, to find out what he was doing wrong, to build bridges and here he was having an invitation made to him that was a struggle to refuse. As he was trying to compose himself to make a reply, he felt his suit pocket vibrate. His phone was ringing.

"Sorry, just let me get this." As he reached into his suit pocket Sheila shrugged acceptance, lifting her glass to her red lips. The caller identification was Linda's mobile: his wife was calling him.

"Hello, darling." Sheila looked bewildered. "What's up?" he asked. There was a period of nodding, followed by, "Just having a drink with a client, could be home in about an hour." More nodding, then a smile! His eyes shone. "Look forward to it, love you." The handset was returned to the suit pocket.

"That was Linda." Sheila shrugged as if it was obvious. "She's been working with her boss on a project that is now finished and, as it is now complete, she has told him that she is leaving to spend more time with me, and she said that if I am home in an hour she will be waiting." The smile broke into a grin. He looked at what was left of his G&T and shook his head. "Not for me, got to go. I'll settle the tab at the bar, Sheila." He rose to go, buttoning his jacket as he did so.

Sheila remained seated. "No need to settle the bill," she said, "I have charged it to the room. The room I thought we might have used but...." He touched her lightly on the shoulder, feeling the texture of the merino wool dress, the dress that he had thought about peeling off her not so long ago. "Thanks, Sheila," was all he said as he headed for the door.

Sheila took another sip of her G&T, turned her head around to survey the bar and caught the eye of a forty something in a suit. Maybe the room would be useful after all.

Note: This is really a story about miscommunication and misunderstanding by all concerned. I wanted to create a tableau where the main character is lost and confused regarding his wife, however due to his misunderstanding of the situation he cannot speak to her and seeks advice elsewhere. His judgment of where to seek that advice is monumentally wrong resulting in him being tempted to have an affair, or at least a fling. His lucky escape is when his wife, who has understood what has been going on calls him.

THE LIGHT OF THE SILVERY MOON

BY LAWRENCE WHALLEY

I knew him at once. Sitting on the top of the wall at the edge of the forest, his heels high in the air and spinning on the peak of his hat. Catching him wasn't difficult but I had heard so many times that the taking of a leprechaun was the easy part. Getting him to do what you want, now that can be very awkward. But I can be just as tricky. My story will tell you how a little girl outwitted a crafty devious old leprechaun and how she got a wonderful Christmas present that she treasures to this day.

You've never seen a leprechaun? They used to be very common all over Ireland. Now the cities are bigger and people are building everywhere there's not many places you can find them. My dad says they live mostly underground now, mending shoes and, of course, counting their gold. That's what they are really good at. No, not counting gold but finding it. Finder's keepers is what they sing to themselves. Not to anyone in particular because they are almost always alone. Come to think of it they're almost always men, old men at that. Do you know, I've never heard of anyone who met a lady leprechaun? Funny that, but there must be an explanation.

My leprechaun – I can say that because I've just caught him - is about three feet tall, and is wearing a neat little red jacket with red breeches buckled at the knee, black stockings and a hat, cocked in the style of a century or two ago. Looking closely, I can see he has a little, old, withered face – a bit like grandpa. There are frills of lace around his neck and at his wrists. Now I see him more closely he looks like one of those men from the time of Shakespeare or the very first Queen Elizabeth. My leprechaun is much better dressed than the first one I saw in Donegal.

I was out walking with mum and dad and my big brother, Oisin.

The leprechaun was sitting on the shore staring out to sea. It was on the wild, west coast of Ireland where the great Atlantic Ocean has winds that bring almost constant rain. He didn't wear lace and stuff, just an enormous overcoat over his pretty red suit. My brother Oisin would have passed him by, but not me. I spotted his cocked hat and I knew who was underneath. That one tricked me and got away. He gave me a choice in return for his freedom. "You can have three wishes or a crock of gold" he'd said. Of course, I took the three wishes and that was my big mistake. He was so clever he tricked me.

My first wish was for all his gold, lots of it. And Lo! there it was all around me in piles so big I couldn't count it. Next, I asked that Ireland should be turned into a tropical paradise with wonderful fruits, sandy beaches, sunshine and a fountain that sprinkled white wine spritzers into silver cups. It was exactly like that, but after a little while I realised that I was the only person living in Ireland. There were no shops where I could spend my gold and worse I only had what I was wearing when I caught the wee fellow. I wasted my third wish asking him to take me home, back to Ireland!

They'll be no mistakes this time. I'll not be as greedy as before and just ask for one crock of gold and let him go on his way.

So here I am by the wall at the edge of the forest. I've been here a few hours now. I can't take my eyes off him otherwise he'll escape. But worse, you see, a crock of gold is not like a bag of shopping. Gold is really heavy. I can't carry it. I can't hide it – that leprechaun is sure to be watching and will take it back as soon as I'm gone for help.

It's beginning to get dark. Lucky there's a full moon tonight and it's not too cold even though it's December. The wee fellow started to sing a few minutes ago. I didn't recognise it at first but I do now.

"By the light of silvery moon" he sings

"To this colleen I'll croon my golden tune

Golden moon, bring back my dreams

This ain't what it seems

It"ll be all mine soon

By the silvery moon."

Leprechauns are great ventriloquists, I can still keep my eyes on him but I want to turn around and see where the singing is coming from. I stay as stiff as I can and stare at him. "Would you like a Christmas present?" he asks at the end of his song. "I have new shoes for you, so comfortable and beautiful too."

I know he's a great cobbler and I just love shoes. I have some I never wear. I just look at them so I nearly said 'yes'. But I didn't. I'd heard this was a leprechaun trick. They would be magical shoes so if I put them on, he'd make me look a fool, make me run, jump and fall over.

"These shoes I have are just fine" I told him with a stern face, still staring at him.

"That's a shame" he complained "I'm such a good cobbler. Tell you what, I'll just have to play you a little tune on my bagpipes."

"Oh no you won't" and I jumped up and snatched the pipes from him. "Everyone knows this is another of your tricks. You'll make me dance so much I won't stop until I'm in the next county!"

I scratched my head and racked my brains. What could I do? "Don't be greedy" that was my mistake last time. If I can't carry all the gold that doesn't mean I can't carry some of it. I will need to compromise, negotiate. So I said to him "Aren't your friends looking for you? Won't you be missed? You're too small to be out at night by yourself!"

He looked even crosser than when I first caught him. "Maybe but you don't know leprechauns. They would just laugh at me for getting caught. They would say you're entitled to my gold. Probably help you take it home."

"That's terrible" I sounded very sincere, almost sympathetic. "My family will be out looking for me right now. On such a bright night so near Christmas they're sure to find me any minute."

He began to look very sad. "When the other leprechauns come out after you've gone they'll poke fun at me" he almost wept.

"That's terrible" I tried to comfort him, "look, there must be a way out of this before my family get here and take you captive."

"Argh!" he screamed "I'll end up in a circus as a dwarf or something worse!" baring his clenched teeth and stabbing his fist in front of him.

I looked at him in my very best serious way. "Just stop that, it's terrible." I was very severe. "Let me think" and I put my finger on my chin and stared at him even harder. "I know, I'll give back half the gold to you and you can say you tricked me out of it and the other half I'll keep, if you don't mind."

He seemed perplexed "erm, half each that's not too bad, let me think about that."

"Just count yourself lucky" I said "I get only half of what even a leprechaun can see I'm entitled to and you're saved all that embarrassment. In fact, you can claim a lucky escape, sort of."

I don't know if you've ever seen a leprechaun smile. It's not pleasant. It's as though they've just eaten a small child and are filled with self-satisfaction such is their evil nature. So we agree to divide the crock. He does a bit of a disappointing dance around his share and I gather up mine to say goodbye.

"You've been so kind to me" he speaks with a trace of shyness. "I shall give you a Christmas present that you'll never see. Intrigued, I wondered what that could be. "When you are older and with someone you really love and your face is caught in the light of the silvery moon, you will become the most beautiful girl in Ireland."

And it was true. There are magical moments when my face catches the light of the moon and my husband can't take his eyes away from me.

THE LION

BY HILARY COOMBES

At first she didn't realise that she and the lion had a common need. They were both searching.

The lion was searching for food. She? For freedom. Freedom from this hellhole. Freedom from the constant drudgery.

It would be a matter of time – for the lion. For her? Who knew?

She spied him on the horizon. Menacing. Prowling. Watching her.

She stood on the porch. The African prairie grass now burned to a crisp was no longer food for man or beast.

The man would be home soon, flagon of beer tied to the horse. He'd demand food. He'd demand the use of her body. She looked at her bruises. She shivered. No more. Please no more.

She gently rubbed her hand over her distended stomach. The baby was safe inside, just about. No doubt he'd join the others in the little makeshift graveyard outside the hut. Hunger got them all in the end.

The lion moved cautiously nearer. She moved indoors, carefully bolting the wooden door. Carefully putting the wooden slats across the window. Would it be enough? Enough to keep him out?

Her eyes adjusted to the light of the scorching sun peeping through the wooden window slats. No sign of the lion but she could hear him. His breathing was louder than his footsteps on the porch.

His rancid smell pushed its way into the hut as the Lion paced the porch. She knew that unless he ate soon he'd be meat for the carrions. She vomited. Perhaps it was her remains that the carrions would enjoy.

To be his dinner might give her the freedom for which she was searching. Should she open the door? Please God it would be a quick death. She needed it to be quick.

She crouched back in the darkness of the corner. Thinking.

Her body jumped at the loud crack of the gun. She hadn't heard the man's horse approach.

She heard the lion's woeful roar. She covered her ears. Desolation wrapped her tightly like a blanket.

She imagined the lion no longer searching. His body crumpled on the porch. His hunger at peace.

Tears fell. For the lion or for herself? She didn't know.

She expected the man to bang angrily on the door very soon. She shivered despite the immense heat.

Her baby pushed angrily within her womb. She wished she could push away her shacklcs in the same way, but the only escape for her would be death.

She wished she could return to her family. They had no idea what had become of her. They had no idea of the cruelty of the man.

How long she crouched in the dark she'd never know. Minutes felt like hours. She was almost in total darkness. The sunlight through the slats almost gone.

Crawling to her feet she tried to see through the slats. Nothing. Only blackness. Carefully, hesitantly, she unbolted the door.

Blood seeped around the entrance. The lion was at peace. He hungered no longer.

She noticed the horse searching in vain for a living blade of grass. He wasn't tied. He was free. She would join him.

She pulled herself up on his back. He was too hungry, too tired to complain. Together they plodded away from the hellhole that had imprisoned her for too long.

She looked back. The dead body of the man lay on the porch. His heart and lungs now fueling the needs of the unseen lion that had returned to the savannah.

She smiled.

It was over.

She was going home.

NOTE: This was my entry for a writing competition organised by Bay Radio, a Mediterranean coast broadcasting station, which has a large international audience online across the world as well as being live on air in Spain.

I have no idea where the idea of writing 'The Lion' came from, but I know it can still bring a lump to my throat when I reread it.

It won first prize.

MAN FOR HIRE

BY DOT GARRETT

Richard was a charming man. It oozed from every pore. He was not particularly handsome. He had often been compared to Dustin Hofman and, at 5' 7", he was not tall. He had S.M.S - that 'small man syndrome' that often convinced people that he was more important than he actually was. Richard was also a psychopath: he felt no guilt. That particular gene was missing from his psyche.

At 64 years old Richard had perfected the art of lying. He knew he needed a very good memory to be an accomplished liar. Really he should have been an actor; he had perfected the various roles he had taken on over the years.

He could be Dick, the man's man, everyone's friend; witty riposte's and banter with the lads. That was until he made a move on the most attractive wife at the party.

Rick was the lovable rogue, always ducking and diving. All the women loved a bad man, a bit of rough.

And when he was Richard, his given name, he was the sophisticated business man, an entrepreneur. No one knew how many businesses he was involved with but he carried an air of success. With his hand made suits and Italian leather shoes he generally arrived with a young, tall, blonde on his arm. Arm candy he called them, they would cost him money though, so he generally left with an ageing, giggling widow. He could charm them into bed and part them from a few grand on the way out.

However, Richard was struggling. 64 was old but not old enough. He had never put anything aside for his old age, living for the day, for the thrill. He was tired. Possibly because as his last role, in his persona of Dick, he had failed miserably to rise to the occasion on a couple of nights and Joan had come to the conclusion that keeping him in the comfort to which she required was not worth the considerable amount it was costing her in widow's pension. He was shown the door. He couldn't understand it. He always did the leaving.

It was time for a change. As he sat in the bar of The Crown public house, cradling a pint, he was feeling decidedly sorry for himself.

"How's it going, Dick?" Richard looked up to see Steve. Steve ran the franchise of a local estate agent and had found a room for Richard to rent in a not so salubrious part of town but beggars can't be chooser's, eh? Richard had told Steve that it would only be a short term rent as he was sure he would be taken care of again soon.

"Do you need to extend the lease on that room?" Steve asked.

"Yeah, I'm still waiting on a start date for the new position out of town," Richard lied. "I will call in later to sign for a couple more months. Come and sit down and let me buy you a pint".

Richard indicated to the bar man to bring them two more pints over. "So, how's the real estate business going?" Richard asked.

"Not bad at all," replied Steve "I had an interesting sale this week, as a matter of fact. An elderly couple bought a house. They had been living in Spain, still got the villa and said they would keep it for holidays and for the kids to use."

"Alright for some" muttered Richard,

"Tell me about it" replied Steve "Would you believe, they are only back in England because the wife wants to be near the Grandchildren. I know where I would rather be, if I had the choice." He smiled. "Actually," he added "they are looking for a house sitter. Seems they are not going back as they want to be here for the birth of their first great grandchild and they have two rescue dogs back in Spain. It will take time for the dogs to get clearance to come back to the UK, some kind of pet passport."

"Really!" exclaimed Richard. "I would be up for that. I Could do with a break in the sun before I start the next job."

"They want references," said Steve.

"No problem" replied Richard; he always had a stock supply on his laptop ready to print out when the occasion arose and, when someone rang to confirm his glowing report, the number he had supplied was one of his many 'pay as you go' phones kept for this reason, although, in his experience, not many people actually followed up references.

"OK, call by the office later this afternoon and we can get the ball rolling," said Steve, finishing off his pint and getting up to leave.

Richard left the pub with a new spring in his step - just what he wanted; a new challenge - and he would start working on his new persona right away. "Ricky," he thought, "just like Ricky Martin, the Spanish heart throb. Watch out senoritas! Here I come!"

Six months later Ricky was catching some rays by the pool and thinking how that chance meeting in the pub had changed his life, best pint he had ever had to pay for, he was even contemplating marriage to the lovely Maggie.

"Ready for a G&T" called Maggie from the naya

"Sounds good to me" replied Ricky "I'll just pick a lemon off the tree shall I"

"Yes please" said Maggie.

As he pulled himself off the sun lounger Ricky thought about Maggie. Not the youngest of the bunch, they had all rushed to be his friend when he had arrived in Moraira, seems there was a shortage of eligible, solvent men for all the widow's and divorcees in this town. But Maggie was vivacious and very attentive to his needs; she also gave him space, time for himself, as she worked most mornings. She had found a good niche here with her insurance company, selling to the expats and they were queuing up to buy her funeral plans.

"Man for hire" he chuckled to himself remembering his first plan when he had arrived in Spain, all the women needed a "handyman" and then all he had to do was choose the one who provided a nice villa and a welcoming bed. He had moved out of the old couples place when the dogs were shipped over to England, although by then as well as his plan he had a good resume for Ricky. Early retirement due to health reasons and just waiting for the proceeds from the sale of his house in England to come through was the general story and he was vague about the rest of his past. Mainly the women he met were not that curious, often they had been starved of attention and only wanted to talk about themselves, Ricky was a good listener.

In the two months he had spent dog sitting he had put an advert in the local expat free papers offering his services to lonely women as an escort. He had been an immediate success, always immaculately dressed for the occasion, a good mover on the dance floor and he had them all swooning. Maggie had seemed the best bet for his long term plans, which were basically just to relax in the sun, so after she asked him to move in and give up his "day job" he had been happy to oblige.

Now, as he sipped his drink, he looked around him and thought life couldn't get much better.

Maggie's voice broke through his revere "Ricky, how do you fancy a trip out next week" she said "there are local fiestas and I have to close the office for two days"

"Where do you fancy going babe" asked Ricky.

"We could take a picnic and drive up into the mountains, I know a nice spot and we can take a walk to see a waterfall" she said

"Sounds lovely" replied Ricky, he could think of nothing worse, much preferring to laze by the pool, "got to keep her sweet though Ricky boy" he secretly thought.

The following week Maggie and Ricky were relaxing on the picnic blanket, gazing at a clear blue sky, they could even see eagles soaring high above the peaks of the mountain. "You did us proud babe, the picnic was great, lovely tapas and cava" said Ricky, slurring slightly as he had drunk most of the wine, Maggie had said she would drive back.

"Shall we take that walk now?" asked Maggie

"Before we do I have something to ask you" said Ricky, "oh, what's that then" said Maggie, fluttering her eyes. Ricky took a deep breath "I was wondering if you would do me the honour of marrying me" he said and then took Maggie in his arms kissing her he murmured "please say yes".

Breathless, Maggie looked hard at Ricky and said "oh, that came as a surprise, I do love you but I need some time to think about it"

"That's ok," said Ricky "but please don't take too long to think, we are not getting any younger and I have waited a long time to find my soul mate" he felt quite confident that she would say yes and then he wouldn't have to pretend anymore.

"I promise I won't take long" said Maggie, adding "Let's take that walk now".

As they walked along the track that was winding steeply upwards Ricky found himself stumbling, what with the hot sun and the wine he felt a bit woozy "how much further babe?" he asked,

"Not far now, just up around that next bend" Maggie replied.

As they squeezed through a gap in the rocks Ricky suddenly found himself above a very steep drop, a ravine. "Careful here babe" he said.

Maggie stood a couple of steps before him and said in a very quiet voice "No Richard, it is you who needs to be careful" Ricky found it hard to concentrate on what Maggie was saying, why had she suddenly got a look in her eye that had not been there before

"What do you mean" he asked.

"I know all about you Richard Watts, all your lies, you can find out a lot of things on the internet these days, thought you would have a meal ticket with me did you?"

"I don't know what you mean Maggie" stuttered Ricky "I love you babe, you love me too, we are soul mates".

"Let's go back now" said Ricky, suddenly feeling panicky.

Maggie put her hands out and gave Ricky a gentle push, as he staggered backwards she said "The only place you are going Ricky is straight to hell" and as Richard felt himself falling down, down into the ravine he heard Maggie shout "Never kid a kidder, they didn't call me Margaret Brown the Black widow of Bicester for nothing." Then he crashed onto a boulder and thought no more.

As Maggie drove back to Moraira she knew she had put on the best performance of her life, calling the police and waiting for them to arrive, then having Richard airlifted out, his body still and lifeless she had cried and sobbed at the sudden loss of her fiancé. All she had to do now was put in the claim for the life insurance she had taken out for Richard a couple of months earlier and she would have the life she wanted, relaxing by the pool, maybe a cruise, and she certainly did not need to pay for the company of a man for hire.

Note: Based on a real life experience! Much of my writing comes from past memories and feelings, however being part of the group has pushed me to use my imagination and it's very rewarding to find that I can create something entertaining from sometimes serious subjects.

A COUNTRY WALK

BY CAROLYN SIMS

The bus driver crunched through the gears as he pulled away from the unmarked bus stop. Only local villagers would use the stop so it was unnecessary to raise a pole to advertise the spot. Olive Anderson turned her head away from the cloud of exhaust fumes but she was not quick enough to avert her mouth and nose from the toxic cloud which enveloped her. As usual, she coughed and spluttered into her hand for the first few steps she made along the narrow road to her home.

Station Road joined the main road to Alnmouth at a small T junction. The road was not tarmacked, but was reasonably smooth with pot holes at regular intervals which caught the unwary. Olive walked this road twice a day. The first, early in the morning, when she caught the 7.30am bus to Amble and her employment at the hairdressing salon owned by Mr Taylor. Being a country girl, she was used to the long walk from her home to the bus, and then the return journey on the bus and the walk, often in the dark, five days a week. She usually trudged homeward at about 7.00pm, having spent at least half an hour helping to tidy and clean up the salon after a long day on her feet. Now she was an "Improver" she no longer had to clean basins and drains, brush and wash the floor or wash and dry towels as she had done as an apprentice.

She was responsible for checking stock, consulting forward bookings to estimate future stock requirements and alert Mr Taylor of any booking problems such as timings for Marcel waves and hair colouring.

She loved her job. It was what she wanted to do from the age of fourteen when she begged her parents to find her an apprenticeship in one of the local towns. She knew and appreciated the financial sacrifice this entailed for her parents. They had to pay the indenture fees plus the solicitor's fee. For the first year she would earn nothing, require her bus fares, clothing and to be fed. Her father had a safe but poorly paid job as water bailiff for the local gentry. Extra money was made training gun dogs, fattening the pig, and her mother's egg money.

But now in the last year as an "Improver" she was beginning to have her own clients who requested her by name and the tips were often generous when the "county" types visited their country retreats. She had a responsibility to the business to look immaculately coiffured and neatly dressed. Recently she had allowed her allocated apprentice, Sheila, to bleach the front of her dark brown hair, blonde. The other girls in the salon had gasped in surprise, and with a little envy, when they saw the result copied from one of the trade magazines. Olive's parents disapproved, considering dyed hair "fast". She hoped others would not think it too startling for a small country town. Sheila was proud and grateful that her mentor had enough confidence in her ability to risk such a departure from the norm. Mr Taylor had applauded the result and allowed Olive to have the chemicals used at trade price. He wasn't mean, but as he always said "Someone has to pay".

Standing in high heels all day, every day, exacted a high price on the state Olive's legs and feet. Trudging up the road in the twilight and darkness of the winter she tried not to think of the ache of her feet and throbbing of her calf muscles. Of course, she left the glamorous foot wear in her cubbyhole in the staff room, but the sensible walking shoes she now wore only stopped her turning her ankle on the rough surface of the road.

She pulled her coat more tightly around her but the style and quality were more in the eye of the beholder, rather than offering any real protection from the cold or wind. Her father told her she should have purchased a good stout tweed overcoat, rather than the padded shoulder, swing coat she had chosen. Little did he know, had she been able to afford another ten shillings she would have been seduced by the styles sporting a fur collar.

The wind was pulling at her hat and hair, and all the attempts she made to re-pin the hat seemed to be useless. She tried to pull the brim down and the collar of her coat up to her ears, but the wind found its way down her neck with its icy fingers.

"Oh no!" She groaned, "not snow, not tonight". She tried to extract her umbrella from her shopping bag. Her mother insisted she carried it along with her lunch tin, "just in case". But the wind, and the sleet it blew along with it, was difficult to anticipate. One minute it blew in her face, the next from her right and then her left. The umbrella was a hindrance, and she contemplated collapsing it to see if she could make better progress without it. Suddenly, an extremely strong gust of wind decided the matter for her. The umbrella turned itself inside out, and was no use to man or beast.

Olive clung onto it trying to protect it from further damage in the hope that her father would be able to right it for her. She couldn't afford another.

As she fought against the wind and snow flurries she became aware of a movement behind the wall in the field to her right. She couldn't see anything but it sounded as if someone, or something, was trying to climb over the dry stone wall. No one else would be out in this weather. She was accustomed to the sounds of the countryside, but this was unlike the usual animal noises. The wind and snow were beginning to make small drifts across the road, swirling and dancing before her, mocking her determined trudging along the road.

Although the snow distracted her, she was conscious of a cough from behind the wall. Then another, a deep throat clearing cough. "Pull yourself together, Olive my girl", she muttered to herself. She glanced at the stone wall and as she did so a stone was dislodged and dropped from the top of the wall and landed with a soft thud in the snow at the bottom in the ditch. Someone was trying to climb over. Frantic scrabbling consumed her attention, and then a head appeared, only to disappear just as suddenly. It was a sheep trying to find shelter from the snow. Her relief was palpable. Stupid animal, did it not realise there was more shelter in the lea of the wall. She had always thought a sheep's cough more human than animal, but in the snow and wind sound becomes distorted and the senses confused. The familiar turns threatening if you allow your imagination too much latitude.

She re-pinned her hat again and started walking. Peering through the snowy gusts she thought she could see a figure walking towards her. She couldn't be more delighted or surprised. The figure confidently striding along the road with a four legged, black companion. He had a thumb stick in his right hand and the black Labrador at his heel. Olive shouted out with pleasure and relief, "Dad I'm here". As she said it she realised it was totally unnecessary, her father had excellent distance vision, and with the wind at his back had a better chance to see ahead.

Jet, the dog, bounded through the snow flurries to greet her, and sat at her feet like a downed pheasant.

"Your Ma was fretting, so I thought we would have a walk out to check you were managing through the snow. Take my arm, pet, and we'll be home before you can say Jack Robinson."

My mother often talked about her life as a country girl and this story is constructed from various tales she told me about her training as a hairdresser in Northumberland. It didn't sound much fun to me, but she was so grateful to her parents and the sacrifices they made for her apprenticeship.

THE MAZE

BY ROSEMARY SHEPPARD

I've only got myself to blame. I'm totally aware of that, but it doesn't make it any better, quite the reverse in fact. I simply don't see any way out of the situation I find myself in and that makes me frustrated and then angry and then scared, not a sensation I am familiar with and I don't like it one bit. I look into the future and I see my life stretching away into a pointless existence, a totally futile life, lived in the public eye as a pariah, and I can't escape it.

I remember the first time I felt like this, well, something like this. Ernest and I had not been an item for very long when he suggested we might have a day on the river at Hampton Court. We motored down with a picnic and after we had done the palace he suggested that we just had to go into the maze. I remember not being so keen on the idea but Ernest was all in favour so in we went. I thought it all rather juvenile but we strolled around and had been there only a couple of minutes when I turned to say something to him and he had gone. I couldn't see him through the hedges so I called out to him and could hear him laughing, giggling really, and that made me mad. I called out something to the effect that I would wait for him at the entrance and he laughed once more and I was on my own.

Well, try as I might I could not get out of that damn maze. I thought at first it was just going to be a question of retracing my steps but quickly realised that I had been paying all too scant attention to the steps we had taken. I stood stock still and thought and then tried using logic but it was all to no avail. Wherever I turned I saw a dead end in front of me, until my entire vision was green foliage. My pace quickened and finally I was running down the lanes between the impenetrable hedges, in my desperation to get out, the memory of Ernest's laughter ringing in my ears. I felt my frustration and anger mounting to such an extent that to my horror I realised that I was close to tears. I couldn't remember having cried before, even as a child. I had always been in command of myself, always gone for what I wanted and got it. Tears have no place in that philosophy. I suddenly felt that I was going to scream the place down, become totally hysterical. I felt claustrophobic and helpless and undignified and it was altogether the most awful experience of my life.

I can't really remember how I got out but somehow I did, only to find Ernest waiting for me, smoking a cigarette and talking to some woman. The journey back to London was, to say the least, not a happy one and my displeasure with him lasted for several weeks. It wasn't until he had sent me daily bouquets of flowers and made me several gifts of very expensive jewellery that I relented and let him back into my bed but I never, ever let him forget it, and he never, ever again tried to make fun of me.

David buys me very expensive jewellery, lets me have anything I want, in fact, in return for what I provide for him. He is very generous and I do feel very fond of him but how I shall feel when the situation has changed, I don't really know. Well, that's not strictly true; I do know and that is half of the trouble, that and the fact that the very thing I had aspired to has been snatched from my grasp and is lost to me for ever.

I well remember the first time I met David. Thelma arranged it for me. I was curious to meet him and, of course, I did have it in the back of my mind to steal him away from her and Freda.

I was thirty five at the time and well aware that I was no beauty but I was always elegance personified and I had other talents, acquired in various parts of the world, under various gentlemen of various nationalities. I knew that men found my conversation, my sense of humour and my general demeanour utterly captivating. It's so easy to flirt oneself into bed with any man if you go about it the right way, and I had done rather a lot of that.

So I was introduced to David and he proved to be as good looking and charming as I had been led to believe. Over the next few months Ernest and I were included in many house parties at which David was a guest and I had the chance to study him carefully and lay my plans. He became used to seeing us and we became part of his inner circle. I decided to present myself as utterly un-phased by his rank and position and treated him almost as an inferior, getting him to fetch and carry things for me etc. virtually showing him contempt but in a respectful way, if that makes any sense.

He seemed to relish this very unconventional approach, never having encountered anything like it before in the circumstances which surrounded his life, and he gradually singled me out more and more until finally we came to an understanding and our relationship became a sexual one.

It was then that I realised what was going to be required of me in that department. David was not quite as other men, oh, not impotent or of the 'other' persuasion but his upbringing in the hands of indulgent nannies and parents who had been distant and even cruel in their dealings with their children had left him needful in certain directions. I knew that to maintain our relationship I was going to have to cope with these needs, do certain things, perform certain acts which would turn him on and keep him coming back for more. I didn't particularly relish the idea – it's not my natural instinct to behave in that way, but big rewards beckoned to me and I gritted my teeth and did the necessary. I realised that it would have been virtually impossible for him to have met a woman in the circles he moved in who would be willing to carry out these acts for him, and, in his position, prostitutes would not have been a viable possibility. In view of all this, it was no surprise that I soon became indispensable to him and he declared himself mine until death. He became, in short, totally besotted with me.

The fringe benefits of this relationship were enormous. I became his hostess as well as his mistress and those in the know were made to accede to me. This particularly galled his sister in law, the tubby little Scottish woman whose dislike of me shone forth from her eyes whenever we met, though her husband Bertie, David's younger brother, was always unfailingly polite if a little distant towards me.

I regarded them both with utter contempt, as I did his entire family.

Our life together was very pleasant, one long round of parties in fact. I loved the power that my association with him gave me. I felt that I had finally reached the position that I had been born to and had aspired to all my life. David was more than generous, constantly lavishing gifts upon me and we were continually going on holidays to exotic places. Naturally Ernest had to tag along wherever we went together. He was, after all, still my husband and appearances had to be maintained even if our intimate life had ceased several years earlier. He had long since provided himself with his own little friend to take care of his needs in the bedroom department. As for my own sexual needs, well they were scarcely being filled by the part I had to play with David, but he was actually most understanding and turned a blind eye when I felt the need to take a lover myself, something I did in a very discrete manner.

No, life was most enjoyable and I could just sit back and wait for the day when his father would die and David would become King. Then I should really come into my own.

When David became King we were ecstatic. I had divorced Ernest earlier in the year and I was free to marry David as soon as possible. I would be Queen, Queen Wallis, and I would be the most stylish and elegant queen that Britain had ever had. I began to act the part, in private – naturally. Most of the country knew nothing of my existence, of their darling new King's total reliance on an American divorcee, but the people would love me because he loved me. I used to laugh to myself at that. The British are so stuffy, so set in their ways.

There would have to be some changes made in the way things were done and I was just the person to see that those changes were made. David would do everything I asked of him. The future, my future, was assured.

Nothing ever turns out as one expects. I should have known that. I should have realised that the petit bourgeoisie which runs the country would not allow him to place a divorced woman on the throne, but I simply didn't understand. David had told me that he would prevail, had promised me that he would get what he wanted once he was King, his immense popularity in the country would sweep the old thinking out of the way forever and I had believed him. The whole of Europe is changing. Surely Britain would not want to face the future ruled by a stammering no-body with a plump little hausfrau beside him when they could have our grace and elegance at the helm. It was beyond belief, IS beyond belief.

I had not taken into account the power of the Church and the Establishment, the moguls in Whitehall, the blessed Empire, his bloody mother, even, it turned out, his beloved subjects. When faced with the prospect of someone they obviously thought of as the whore to end all whores on the throne, the whole pack of them collapsed into their own version of hysteria and it was made abundantly clear to David that he had to choose between me and being King.

To my utter horror and amazement, he chose me. Now, what a pretty kettle of fish that has lain before me. Surely, once crowned, he could have had his cake and eaten it, so to speak, but no! The bloody man has decided that he wants to marry me and so he had to be totally British and up front about it all and has turned his back on all the power and the glory. Where does that leave me, for God's sake? I cannot leave him. That is completely out of the question. How could I retake my place in society if I leave the King? I am forty years old and my days of catching the eye of potential wealthy lovers are almost at an end. Besides, I have no money of my own. How would I live? Ernest did not bestow vast sums of money on me on our divorce - we needed to get it all over with as quickly as possible and with a King at my beck and call I hardly needed financial stability. My impoverished childhood taught me that money is everything and. besides, there is simply so way that I can live in any fashion other than the one I have become accustomed to. I won't do it. I can't do it.

So that leaves me with David – for ever it would seem; with a child-man for whom I feel some measure of affection but not the grand passion that he entertains for me. He doesn't seem to have realised it yet but his decision is going to leave us on the outskirts of the very society we have become accustomed to leading. I know that all our 'so-called friends', the British aristocracy, will adopt a hypocritical and holier than thou attitude, and will close ranks against us. We shall be banished to eternal exile, shall be for ever on the outside looking in, while that nincompoop and his poxy wife will be lording it in London.

How can I bear it? How can I bear it? I could scream the place down. She who would be Queen will become an object of scorn, of derision even, remembered for all time as 'that woman', the woman who stole the British King. My name will become synonymous with evil. I see it all so clearly now. How could I have got it all so wrong? I long to extricate myself from this mess that I have brought upon myself but there is nothing I can do. Nothing! I have no choice. I see the hedges of that damn maze closing round me once more and this time there is NO way out.....

Note: This story is my interpretation of an episode in British History which is known to everyone. In this case the lucky escape was experienced by Britain and its Empire but the narrative also depicts a situation where the main character finds herself with no escape at all. The maze incident is my invention but the rest of the story is based on fact.

CONSERVATION OF DESTINY

BY OWEN SUTHERLAND

The day did not get off to a good start

But would you want it to – think of the consequences

Remember the Law of the Conservation of Destiny

Fortune may be transformed temporarily

But overall its balance cannot be disturbed

It will always compensate and be conserved

Good luck will require a measure of bad

Millions of mishaps will begat someone good fortune

A lottery with winners and losers but no Camelot

Thousands who labour long hours on low pay

Will produce a plethora of cheap products for others

Who never question the lot of those making their luck.

Disasters are made by innumerable minnows

With smidgens of blessings fractions of flukes

All combining in one inevitable eruption of evil

But then like a volcano from out of its fire

Come fertile ashes spread far and about

And good will grow for the masses without.

Something that's good may come from delay

Where are the car keys they will go astray

Fortune thrives on such moments of luck

Now you're following the wagon not under the truck

Your destiny is preserved without making you scared

So next time you're late remember what you might have been spared.

SAFARI

BY JENNIFER NESTEROFF

"I am not afraid" I told myself.

"Of course you're afraid. You're bloody terrified!" my Inner voice shouted, interfering with my effort to be brave.

My Inner voice, the bane of my life, is forever screwing things up for me. When I decided to get away from my dull city life and do something exciting for once, she was appalled.

"You can't do that. You haven't got the guts!"

Ignoring her, I picked up the Travel Brochure I'd selected from my local agents and scanned the pages. I found what I thought was the very thing.

"I'll go on an African safari!" I declared.

"What?! Now you are being ridiculous. A gentle cruise down the Rhine if you must, but a safari! In Africa! What if you break a nail? Not to mention being eaten by a lion, which, knowing you, would be quite likely to happen."

"Oh, shut up! I've decided and that's that."

Inner voice got the huffs. "Suit yourself, but I wouldn't be in your shoes when it all goes pear shaped. Oh damn, I suppose I will be!"

So, there I was, on Safari in the wilds of Africa.

One morning I had just left my tent to admire the breath taking sunrise in peace before my travelling companions awoke. As I reached the boundary of the camp I became aware of the feeling that something was watching me. I looked about me and suddenly saw it.

"Oh my God, that's a ....!"

"Yep, that's a lion all right, staring straight at you. Remember I warned you about this. What do you think you will do?" My Inner voice was obviously having a great time.

Then, after having a disagreement about whether I was afraid or not, I considered my options and found that turning tail and running seemed favourable.

"Better not do that," chortled Inner voice. "That would be the best way to become an early breakfast before you've even seen the sunrise. May I suggest you stand quite still and let the lion think about what it wants to do? Who knows, it may have had breakfast already."

So there I stood and the lion and I looked at each other until the lion finally yawned and sat down.

"Oh look, you've bored it and that proves my point about you. You've never been very entertaining and now even that lion has lost interest in you."

"Stop it; this is not the time for a character analysis. I wonder if I could move now."

Inner voice considered for a moment, "Perhaps you could back away very slowly, but just don't trip over or the thing might think you are more fun than you looked to be."

I began to move and as I did the lion got up and started to trot towards me.

"Oh no, this is it!" I quavered.

Inner voice seemed to agree as I heard nothing from her other than a small mumbling which might have been a prayer.

Although I had my eyes closed as I waited for the fatal attack, I could swear I heard the lion padding straight past me!

"Good morning, this is a beautiful time of day, isn't it?"

My eyes shot open at the sound of a man's voice. I turned to see our Tour Guide standing behind me, calmly fondling the lion as it licked his hand.

"I see you've met Molly then," he grinned. Great, isn't she? I raised her from a cub and since I've been conducting these tours she has become quite a camp follower."

THE LETTER

BY MADDY PATTERN

Dear George,

I know it's been a very long time since you heard from me, but there's been so much going on here, that I simply haven't had the time. It's quite a long letter as I've so much to tell you.

I've been doing a lot of gardening...mainly looking after the allotment. There are runner beans, peas, potatoes, sprouts and spinach, plus lots of other things. It's hard work but very enjoyable and rewarding. Of course, you never really had any interest in our garden, except to sit out on the patio with the Racing News, your beer and fags, whilst every now and then making snide, crude comments about me on my knees weeding...then laughing away to yourself! Still, I didn't care, I loved the garden and it gave me huge satisfaction to have it looking nice, plus great thinking time.

You'll be pleased to hear I've lost some weight...something you went on and on about, me looking like a beached whale! Well no more! I'm now a size 12 and, though I say so myself, am looking pretty good! Have also had blonde highlights put in my hair. You always liked blondes didn't you? There was the blonde, busty barmaid at The Bull and Bush that you were seen screwing round the back of the pub! Though rumour had it that she was clean shaven and no bush! Haha!

The list of your infidelities was endless. You think I didn't know? Of course I knew! I paid a private detective to follow you on and off for about a year and a half. The reports he gave me I hid in the attic as I knew you never went up there! You're now probably thinking how could I have afforded it? Well I had my secrets too! Little did you know that when my mum died, she left me quite a tidy sum which I put away in a bank which you knew nothing about. I just told you she'd left me bits and pieces of costume jewellery and the old rocking chair she was so fond of. Anyway, I digress...back briefly to your blonde lovers! The straw that really broke the camel's back was, of course, you screwing my blonde, so called best friend, June! That and many other things absolutely did it for me! But, I'll come back to that later on.

Were you aware that the never ending taunts and making fun of me hurt me dreadfully? Were you aware that whenever you came back from the pub drunk and angry, you hit and punched me until I fell on the ground! That time I was in hospital for a minor operation and they wanted to keep me in overnight because of the anaesthetic...but you insisted I was okay, that you would look after me and I should come home...despite my telling you I didn't feel great and the nurses telling you that it wasn't a good idea for me to leave.

You signed the discharge papers, carted me off to the car and drove home, stopping once at the Tesco Express to buy some beers! Whilst you were gone I felt dreadful and had to open the car door where I was violently sick. At home I went straight to bed. Then you came up, poked your head round the bedroom door and said that as I was okay, you were just popping down to the pub for a pint and when you got home you'd make us some supper. This was about 6.30pm...you didn't get home until 11.30pm...when you crawled into bed, drunk and mumbling to yourself. There was, of course, no supper!

You actually never looked after me then, or at any other time! Do you remember the time my mum came to stay and sitting down to eat our supper I accidentally swallowed a pea down the wrong way and started to choke? You sat there laughing your head off and didn't move to help me. It was my lovely mum, although crippled with Rheumatoid Arthritis, who got up and started banging me on my back that helped dislodge the pea! Incredibly, you were still laughing! I thanked my mum, but was so angry I got up and, most unusually for me, went out and down to the pub, where I proceeded to get drunk myself!

Everything was about you and only you. You couldn't pass a mirror without looking into it and fiddling with your hair. The time you came home with blonde highlights in your hair! You thought it looked great and I thought it looked awful! As I'd got to know the signs, knew there was obviously a woman you wanted to impress! It certainly wasn't me!

Now to my best friend June...and I don't blame just you...she was guilty too! She carried on being my friend and, I really thought she was my friend, when all the time she was shagging you behind my back! When I finally found out, she was so nasty to me, saying that I hadn't been a proper wife to you, didn't want sex with you and other horrible things that can only have come from you! She was no friend, just a leech! As for you, why her when you knew she was supposedly my friend? I still shake my head in amazement as to what was the attraction! Apart from being married to a friend of ours, she had a slight moustache, tight curly, fuzzy hair and, when we went swimming at a local pool once a week, I noticed that she had a hairy back too! Really George? Then you got death threats on your mobile and you hid indoors for a couple of weeks in case her husband came to sort you out! Incredible! They say you should never shit on your own doorstep! Haha! You did...just because you couldn't keep your dick in your trousers! You swore to me afterwards that you would never do it again. You arranged for our wedding vows to be renewed...you promised me so much and I believed you. How stupid can one be? Because all through this you'd already started an affair with someone else!

When my mum was dying, even though the hospital she was in was 150 miles away...I begged you to come and be with me so I wasn't alone. I told you I needed you! Did you come to support me? No, you didn't! You made some excuse to do with work!

As I took care of the bills, I remember finding two entries in our bank statement that I didn't know what they were for. When I asked you, you lied about what they were. I, of course, did some research and found out that they were payments for a lap dancing club in Bournemouth, where you'd been twice on business! When I faced you again with what I knew, you finally told me the truth! Then there were the phone bills. You had been ringing sex lines! Really? Wasn't I enough for you? Obviously not! I enjoyed sex with you and was always up for it...yet you needed more!

As for that fateful day in September, when you told me, late afternoon, that you were going with a couple of friends to the beer festival in the local town and I asked you not to go! The row we had over it! I knew exactly what would happen! You'd get absolutely plastered and then take it out on me when you got home. You just told me to fuck off and that you'd do what you want to do and that I always wanted to spoil your fun! It really was a horrible fight, with both of us shouting at each other. You then slapped me across the face and stormed off, slamming the door. I didn't see you again till much later that night.

About 11.30pm, there was a knock on the front door, and your two friends stood in the doorway holding you up, so drunk you couldn't even stand! They carried you upstairs and put you to bed, laying you down on your front in case you threw up! I remember going downstairs to get a bucket in the event you were sick...then going back upstairs to find you had already vomited everywhere, plus you had pissed yourself. I did try to roll you over to put a towel underneath the sheet and one on top for you to lie on...but I couldn't move you! It was at this point, looking down at you, I realised I felt nothing but disgust and pure hatred for you!

What happened next was much of a blur to me! Almost as though I wasn't there and sleep walking! I had hung a picture on the wall that afternoon in the bedroom and had rushed off to answer the phone, leaving the picture hooks and hammer on the dressing table. Now, in a complete haze, I walked to the dressing table, picked up the hammer and went back to the bed. I had felt nothing but a red mist when I brought down the hammer on your head, then on your back...over and over again! Afterwards, I think I stood there for a while, then dropped the hammer and went downstairs. I had a brandy, which brought me to my senses, then rang 999.

By the time the police and ambulance arrived, I had realised what I had done...but, if I'm honest, I really felt no remorse, only relief! The paramedics, on examining you, said they felt a pulse and rushed you off to hospital. I, of course, was arrested and charged with attempted murder.

Whilst awaiting my trial, my solicitor obviously brought me news of your condition. That you had been on life support for some time; then you came round after some months, but that you now remain on a machine to help you breathe! By the time the trial had finished, I'd heard that you'd been moved to a specialist nursing home, where you'll probably be for the rest of your life, however long that might be!

At my trial, your treatment and abuse of me plus the multitude of affairs were brought in mitigation and I had a sympathetic judge and jury. So instead of a life sentence, which I was expecting, was given eight years imprisonment and, taking off time served with good behaviour, I should be released on parole in about three weeks, having now served four years of my sentence.

I'm looking forward to that day. A very close friend of mine, Tom, has been looking after the house and keeping the garden tidy. He visits me every week and brings me food and other bits and pieces. I'm in an open prison now as I pose no risk to the public! We talk about what we're going to do after I go home. He's a kind, caring man who I knew before my attempt to murder you. Oh, yes! I was having an affair of my own! We shall probably get married and, because the house was signed over to me in our divorce settlement, I will sell it. Tom, who's already sold his house, and I will buy another house together somewhere else far away.

Well, I'd better close now and take this to the post point so it can be sent off, along with many of the other prisoners' letters.

I make no apologies for sounding hard and harsh and for what I did to you! You were cruel, abusive and unkind and you almost destroyed me as a person! You were never there for me, ever! You got what you deserved! Truly!

Take care of yourself. I'm sure the nurse will read this to you when she's pushed you out in your wheelchair into the nursing home gardens. It's just one of life's little twists that I only managed to paralyse you from the neck down! At least, you may still have your silly twitchy facial expressions, despite the brain damage! I should have finished you off! But there you are! Some would say you had a lucky escape! I know I did!

From your ex-wife

Sally

LUCKY MAN

BY JOHN ROSS

The metallic taste in his mouth, the ticking of hot metal and the smell of petrol all hit his senses at the same time. "What the f...?" and then he remembered swerving to avoid the deer that had suddenly appeared in the headlights of his silver Vauxhall Vectra. The crunch as the front bumper collapsed, the screech as one of the wheels was almost ripped off as the car hit the verge and launched itself into the hedge, turning as it did so until it landed upside down on the gravel path scoring a huge set of ruts as it careened to a halt. He was hanging upside down, the metallic taste he knew was blood, probably from his nose as the air bag had deployed, he could not feel his right arm and he struggled to release the seat belt with his left.

The day had started in a much more positive note.

As a Territory Customer Relations Manager (TCRM) with DoIT he had worked himself up from the telesales floor to a Territory role and a Company Car. Today was the day for his interview with the Managing Director and the Management Team to sign off his promotion to Regional Manager and he knew that unless he blew it, the job was his.

It meant a cut in his personal bonus plan but a 30%+ increase in his standard salary package and a 20% share of the results of the five TCRMs that he would manage. At the age of 29 he was young and aggressive, and he knew that today would be his lucky day.

Douglas Ian Taylor was the Managing Director of DoIT and the Company name was just one of his Ego trips, he owned a Bentley and an Audi R8, had a 40-foot yacht berthed in Southampton. His 5 bedroom house in Egham was sprawling and the apartment in Menton in the South of France was luxurious. He was also deeply religious. He had been married to Angie for 35 years and they had two sons, neither of whom worked in the business, much to his dismay. It was Douglas that would be chairing his interview that morning.

His name was Peter Davies, he had always had what his Father had called "The Gift of the Gab" in that he could always impress the ladies and talk himself out of trouble. At just over six feet tall with floppy blonde hair and stunning green eyes he had a head start in the world of selling. He left school at 18 with good grades but turned down going to University in favour of making a living. He had tried a couple of jobs until he landed the telesales job at DoIT when he was 20. He had kept his head down and learned how the Company worked, he had clashed with the Floor Manager on several occasions but as his results were better than any three other telesales people he not only got away with it, but he got noticed. It had taken him three years to get from the floor to TCRM and when he was 23 he had been the youngest TCRM the company had ever had.

He developed a taste for Boss Suits, Ferragamo ties and Church shoes but not long-term relationships. His charming good looks and easy style made sure that he was never short of a good-looking woman on his arm, but he felt that there was too much to do and see in the world to settle down. He had a two-bedroom apartment in Churchill Place, in the heart of Basingstoke with a reserved parking space and private access to the Festival Way shopping centre. The increase in money would mean that he could start paying off the mortgage quicker and still have an enjoyable life; luck was still running his way.

As he drove out of the private car park that morning the air was crisp and clean with a hint of frost but azure blue skies, the dash board told him it was 3 degrees with a danger of ice. His drive to the office at Englefield Green would take him 40 minutes unless there was a traffic hold, up as he came off the M3 at Bagshot the SatNav said that all was currently clear. The trip was uneventful and luckily the Bagshot area had indeed been clear. He had driven through Sunningdale, past the entrance for Wentworth Golf Club on his right and the Royal park on his left before he indicated to turn into Wick Road and the office. The DoIT building was three-storeys of concrete and glass set in a park with a number of Victorian buildings around it. The area used to be some sort of stables before the building was erected by DoIT over 15 years ago, it was a peaceful and clean working environment with a large car park and a pleasant feel about it. As he entered the building, Margaret, the receptionist, looked up, "Morning Peter, big day today, good luck."

He waved and said, "thank you," before pushing through the door and walking up the stairs to the third floor and the board room, it was 10:25 and his interview was scheduled for 5 minutes later.

The board room had glass panels and a glass door at the corridor side and a wall of windows on the other side making it a fish tank, and when the sun shone, a warm fish tank. The centre of the room was dominated by the large wooden table with plug sockets and network access points that came up when pressed, he took a seat on the window side in the centre facing the door. He made sure that his mobile phone was switched to silent and waited. Five minutes passed, it was now after the 10:30 appointment, he suddenly thought, "It was the board room wasn't it, not Douglas's office", when Douglas emerged from the lift opposite the door directly in line with Peter. Douglas was a large man, not overly fat but big, he looked like a rugby second row forward who had stopped training, he was 6 feet 4 inches tall with a head of dark ginger hair, neatly cut. A Harris Tweed jacket with a pale blue poplin shirt open at the neck, off white chinos and brown loafers were his attire for the day. Behind Douglas was Andrew, the Sales Director, immaculate in a crisp white shirt, grey suit, red tie, black shoes and black slicked backed hair. Following him was the Finance Director, Robin sporting an inferior Harris Tweed jacket, graph-paper shirt, brown corduroy trousers and brown brogues, all of which was topped off by a mop of unruly dirty blond hair and black rimmed glasses.

Peter stood up as they entered, and they took their seats opposite, Douglas in the middle, Andrew to his right and Robin to his left. "Have you had a coffee Peter?" Douglas asked, his voice tinged with a slight Scottish brogue.

"No, not yet Douglas." Peter replied.

Douglas picked up the telephone handset on the table and punched a few numbers, "Jean we are in the board room, can you bring a pot of coffee, milk and sugar and a plate of whatever biscuits we have at hand?" there was a slight pause then the handset was replaced.

Robin shuffled some papers in front of him, "Now Peter," the heavy Black Country accent with a nasal whine echoed around the room, "Your figures for the last year have been outstanding, however those of your colleagues, or potentially your staff have not. Given the opportunity what would you do about it?" Peter felt 3 pairs of eyes staring at him, but before he could reply the lift pinged and Jean appeared with the refreshments. "Put them on the table Jean, thank you." requested Douglas, the tense atmosphere had been broken and Peter felt relieved.

Cups were filled, milk and sugar dispensed, and biscuits left to lie on the plate. "As Robin asked, what would you do?" the South London voice was Andrew's.

"Well, of the 5 of them I think four are doing a good job but need more focus and direction which I believe I can give, as to the fifth one..."

He was interrupted by Andrew, "And who is the fifth one?" There was steel and bitterness in that short question.

"I think we all know that Ian has been coasting for the last year or so, despite being top sales person a few years ago. I think he has personal issues and we should let him go, there are plenty of new hungry sales people on the telesales floor who would give their right arm to be a TCRM…"

Again he was interrupted by Andrew, "And who would you select Peter?"

"As I do not have the relevant data regarding individual performances or access to their appraisal reviews I honestly could not say at this time but there are three that stand out to me, Alison, Derek and Bill. Every time I have looked at the sales board on the floor they are at or near the top, it has to mean something."

Robin chipped in with, "So you are recommending that we let Ian go, a man who has worked for us for almost 6 years, has been top salesman and has been top team leader…"

It was Peter's turn to interrupt, "If I may say Robin, you have summed it up very well, Ian is a "has been", not a "will be" or an "is."

At this Douglas laughed, "I like your style young man, you've got balls and you've got brains, a trait sadly lacking in so many," as the words left his mouth his head turned ever so slightly to his right, towards Andrew.

Peter took this all in, "Thank you Douglas, my forthright attitude has not always been so welcomed by others," now he was looking at Andrew before coming back to Douglas. "I believe that what is best for the Company has to be the main consideration; we are here to service customers to provide long term security for the staff and shareholders. Ian has been sloppy of late and has lost us at least one account."

"Ah, yes the Condor Account." Douglas pulled himself up straight in the chair, "they have gone out to tender and I want them back, this will be one of the main tasks for the new Regional Manager, do you think you are up to it?"

The question hit Peter like a double-edged sword, of course he had to say yes, but what if he failed? He would become the shortest served Regional Manager in the history of the Company, but then again failure was not in Peter's vocabulary.

"Yes Douglas, it can be done, I know a few of the people there, I am sure that we can get back in and I know that there are two new projects that they have yet to announce..."

Another interruption, "What new projects?" questioned Andrew, "and how would you know about them?"

Peter relaxed in his chair; leaning back he looked Andrew straight in his grey eyes, "I know because I do my research, you know Diane Ford at Condor? The Projects Manager?"

"Yes we all know who she is what about her?"

"Well let's say that she and I had a little dalliance a few weeks ago at the IBM conference and she was trying to impress me with the budget that she had just had approved; £1.85m"

Andrew looked confused, Robin and Douglas both smiled. "And you still have an in with her?" Douglas enquired.

"Absolutely," the smile on Peter's face was difficult to hide.

Douglas looked to his left and then to his right, "Gentlemen, I think we have our new Regional Manager, don't you?" the question did not broach a negative reply.

Chairs were scraped back as everyone stood, "Congratulations Peter," Robin's nasal whine as he walked around the table to shake Peter's hand.

"Thank you Robin."

"Yes, well done Peter, I look forward to an update on the Condor account," this was Douglas already walking out of the door,

"Yes, will do Douglas." Peter answered as Andrew looked at him and turned on his heel after Douglas.

"Payroll will be in touch but as you know, effective now, your salary has been increased by 35% but your personal bonus has been cut by 30%, however the Regional Manager bonus includes 20% for each of the five TCRMs, well four at present as you are no longer one and maybe three shortly."

Robin looked at Peter, who looked back,

"Robin how do I get the appraisals for the three I mentioned and any others that might be worth considering? I need to get replacements in place ASAP so that I can focus on Condor."

"Yes, yes I will sort that out you will have them this afternoon in your new office, however the new Audi A6 will be tomorrow." With that he half turned and waved leaving Peter alone in the board room.

"Regional Manager" he said to himself, "damn, forgot to ask about business cards." He said out loud.

Fastening his jacket, he walked down one floor to the office that would now be his and on entering he found a small cardboard box on the desk, "Wonder what that is?" he thought, picking it up he realised what it was and opened it to find 50 new business cards with Peter Davies, Regional Manager on them. "Forgone conclusion obviously, the interview was just for show."

He put 10 of them into his card holder and threw the old ones in the bin, just as he was about to sit down Penny from HR entered with four manila folders and a single sheet of paper, "Congratulations Peter, well deserved. Here are the staff records that Robin asked me to give you and you need to sign this." She held out the single sheet of paper which detailed his new role, package and responsibilities, it had already been signed by Douglas and Andrew. He signed in the space under them and handed it back. "There you go Pen."

Penny looked at him through her 1960s style winged glasses, "You know Peter nobody has called me Pen for about 35 years." With that she smiled, turned and left the office. Peter was now alone.

He spent three hours reading the appraisals and associated records of the three he had asked for Alison, Derek and Bill plus one other a Michael Spence that Peter did not know. He then rang Penny to arrange to have a 30-minute talk with each of them, the first session started at just after three thirty and finished at quarter to six. He was happy that he would recommend Alison to replace himself and for Bill to replace Ian when they gave him the bad news. He also made a note to discuss Michael with Douglas the next day as he felt that Michael had great potential.

Standing up he realised it had now gone six and made his way to the exit for the car park, opening the door he felt the cutting cold wind and could see small flurries of snow being blown by the wind.

"Should have brought the coat from the car" he said to himself as he ran to the car, pressing the button on the remote to open the door a few yards before he got there. He started up the engine and waited for the air con to start to warm up the inside of the Vectra then he carefully manoeuvred out of the car park and back on to the A30 heading towards home.

He was humming to himself and grinning, grinning so much that he had to look at himself in the rear-view mirror and as he looked back at the road there it was, a deer right in front of him, he braked hard, and the car skidded on the icy surface hit the verge and soared over the hedge to end up upside down in a field.

As he tried to undo his seat belt with his left hand, his right did not seem to work, he felt warm blood starting to run into his eyes from his nose. He struggled from side to side and eventually the seat belt clicked, and he thudded into the upturned roof which was covered in little squares of glass which ripped the shoulder of his Boss suit. He edged his way towards the door, all the time hearing the distant drone of traffic and the ticking of the engine block as it cooled, he could smell the petrol. He tried several times to open the door and had to squeeze himself out of the shattered window. As he fell on the cold gravel he realised that not only was his nose broken, his right arm was too. Slowly standing up he staggered a few paces away from the stricken Vectra and searched for his mobile phone.

As it was in his inside left-hand pocket it was a bit of an ordeal getting it out and as he called 999 for the police and ambulance he thought to himself how lucky he was to be alive but also lucky that it had not happened the day before otherwise he would not have had the interview and lucky that it wasn't tomorrow as he would have totalled a new Audi A6.

Yes, Peter was one lucky guy.

Note: I wanted to write about the need for possessions and status with sales people at all levels but particularly middle and senior management. I also wanted to include the machinations of small company boards, where the owner is the main shareholder and therefore feels he can do as he likes.

The main character is deliberately likeable but detached, calculating and ambitious, traits which allow him to be successful but his normal outgoing and happy manner make him look lucky and a natural at what he does.

His view of luck is that you work hard to make your own luck and his need for possessions and status overrides his other thought processes which is why he lists his lucky escapes in the final paragraph with the top one being that he had not totalled a new car.

STORY TWENTY

FATAL ATTRACTION

BY CAROLYN SIMS

He had caught her eye from the banquette at the back of the bar. She was sitting in the dappled sunshine, her fair hair caught in a tortoiseshell comb at the top of her head. Tendrils of hair had escaped down her neck and around her face either by design or accident he could not tell. When their eyes met she had quickly turned away feigning disinterest but he knew she would look again, her sort always did.

The group of young students were possibly fresher's, full of false confidence and over loud voices and forced laughter. But she was quiet, watchful and uncertain, these new acquaintances, for surely that was what they were, were not long standing friends. All the better he thought; a physically attractive girl would soon have a coterie of friends before the end of the semester. She looked as if she enjoyed a sporty life. Her legs were long and well-toned, slightly tanned as if she had played tennis throughout the summer. Her arms were equally strong and attractively tanned, and her neck. - Well what a neck! He had to quickly produce a handkerchief from his pocket to cover his mouth and the saliva trickling down his chin. He must act quickly before she became tainted, spoiled by the excesses of student life. Where did she live, was she in a hall of residence or one of the many apartment blocks which housed groups of house mates. He hoped the former would be her home. Security was often lax and at the beginning of the term nobody knew who was resident or visitor.

Patience, he told himself, patience, watch and listen. Remain out of the damned sun so no one would get a clear view of him. Handsome men attract attention as much as ugly ones, but it was always worth being cautious and remain alluring to her. He put away the handkerchief and signalled to attract the waiter's attention. He would order one course at a time to give himself plenty of options whether to stay where he was, or quickly exit if she moved on.

The food was good and the anticipation of the chase to come made for a good evening. The sun was slipping down behind the town scape, rays penetrating the side streets and then darkness, that wonderful warm embracing dusk. He was just contemplating ordering a coffee to give himself a shot of caffeine for the night's work when he realised the students and the girl were moving off. Loud bonhomie, air kisses and scraping of chairs accompanied their departure and she made a furtive glance into the back of the bar before leaving with one of the other girls.

"Heigh ho, heigh ho it's off to work we go" he hummed under his breath. Having paid the waiter as quickly as he could he moved out of the bar shadowing the two girls. They were making their way towards the little park often used as a short cut by the town's folk to the residential areas across from the town centre. Silly girls he thought, they obviously did not appreciate how vulnerable they were to flashers, gropers or worse.

He despised such vulgar sexual deviations; his predilection was far more refined and specialized, if he planned the occasion with care.

So it was one of the college residences they were heading for, an old building which he had visited before, unfortunately without any ultimate success – a good chase but poor conclusion. Such was life, but he really needed to be on the ball tonight. Failure would compound his feeling of lassitude and that could not be tolerated for too long. He slipped into the reception area behind a trio of garrulous female students who did not bother to check that the doors had swung shut behind them.

The target was just entering the lift and he could see from the shadowy corner where he hovered that it had stopped on the third floor. Taking care not to meet anyone's eyes he moved with another crowd of mildly drunk students into the lift. One of them produced the required security card and flashing it over the electronic reader – pressed several of the floor buttons as the required numbers were shouted out. No one seemed surprised by his presence, thank goodness for mixed sex halls; they made his life so much easier.

He found a broom cupboard not far from the lift and slipped inside. Patience, patience, waiting for students to settle into their rooms was a bit like waiting for paint to dry. Not that he had had that experience. The girl had disappeared into a room half way down the corridor and now that darkness had enveloped the building his powers were stronger. He slipped from the cupboard and glided down the nearside wall to the door she had entered.

He listened – no sound – he carefully opened the door and eased himself into the room. There she lay in trouble free sleep, hair in a halo around her head and neck; that neck with a gently throbbing carotid artery exposed to his hungry mouth. He gently lowered himself to the bed and bit into her neck. Her eye lids flickered open and a smile played around her lips revealing her large incisor teeth. She pulled him down towards her face and sank her teeth into his neck with a groan of satisfaction.

Not quite what he had envisaged ending the evening, but then sometimes you have to take what you are given.

THE ELEVATOR

BY JENNIFER NESTEROFF

As a social worker I am often required to visit people in the poorer, run down neighbourhoods of the city.

On this occasion I had an appointment to visit as old lady who lived on the sixth floor of a dilapidated council estate building. The entrance hall was dingy and uninviting with a broken light bulb and rubbish strewn on the floor.

Stepping into the lift, I pressed the button, praying that it was not out of order and was relieved to hear it start up and begin its descent. The doors opened when it arrived and I was assaulted by a stale smell of different unpleasant odours which I was determined not to recognise.

Just as I was gingerly setting foot inside, someone appeared from nowhere and followed me in. The stench increased and I glanced at my fellow passenger with distaste. It was a large, bearded young man dressed in clothes that could not have been more filthy. From the corner of his mouth drooped a battered cigarette and as he stood idly scratching the bare skin that protruded from his half open shirt, he turned his eyes on me and commenced staring into my face. I nodded a curt acknowledgment but the man gave no response. He leant against the lift wall and continued gazing at me.

I felt a slow panic beginning to overcome me. Obviously he was someone of unsound mind and although I had been involved with such cases to do with my work, never had I been trapped with such a person as I was now.

I wondered what I might say to start a conversation that would put him at ease but decided not to encourage him for fear of it having the opposite effect.

The lift dawdled noisily on its way upward while I kept my face averted and tried to pretend I was alone. However, I found it impossible to ignore the feeling that he still had his eyes on me and I began asking myself what he was thinking. Did he want to rob or rape me? Did he see me as someone he hated? One unsavoury possibility after the other whirled through my mind.

As we were finally approaching the sixth floor the man moved and out of the corner of my eye I caught the flash of something silver which he was withdrawing from his pocket. I could not stop myself from looking and there in his hand was a small pistol. I froze in horror as I watched him raise it and then closed my eyes. Suddenly I smelt the scent of burning and with a shock of relief I realised what it was. My companion had lit his cigarette with his pistol shaped lighter!

At that moment the lift arrived at the sixth floor and the doors scraped open. I stood for a second trying to recover my wits.

Behind me the man said "After you, pretty lady."

TERROR IN TANGIERS

BY OWEN SUTHERLAND

The alleyway seethes with life of every description.

George, only minutes before, had been safe in his party of tourists being guided around one of Tangiers' bazaars. He had only stopped for a moment to admire a beautifully crafted necklace – maybe a present for his wife. When he looked up he was alone, well hardly alone, but as he craned his neck, scanning the masses, there was no one he knew. Despite the heat George shivered. How was he to get back to the security of his group or to his hotel? He could see the minaret of a mosque, he thought they had been going towards it but wouldn't that way take him deeper into this appalling maze? Surely it would be better to try and retrace his steps back to where they had all left the coach. He decided to go back, it was impossible to hurry; the alleys were narrow and full of people.

People, people everywhere but not a word to speak. After a quarter of an hour, or was it a lifetime, George was getting desperate. He seemed to have no control over where he was going. The alleys seemed to be narrower and busier. They were like the guts of the city pushing George around, grinding him down, squeezing him and digesting his confidence, stripping away his humanity, reducing him to a tattered tangle of threadbare fibres.

George shock himself, he mustn't panic. Keep calm; be logical, he would find a way out. He tried speaking to shopkeepers, saying "Hotel. My hotel, the Holiday Inn?" only to be met with waved arms, smiles and gestures entreating him to enter their shops. He seemed to be going around in circles, both figuratively and literally. There was the minaret of the mosque again, quite close this time. Keep calm, be logical he chanted again. George pulled out his phone and took a photo. He thought he could trace his route if he kept taking photos at every turn. As he moved off he heard a cry and saw someone brandishing his arm at him, shouting at him and coming towards him waving his arm. George turned, he must get away, scared he pushed through the crowd, must get away. Still the shouting and a quick glance back, showed several men not far behind him shouting and waving their arms fiercely at him. What had he done to raise so much anger, cause such offence? Of course, the camera, maybe he had broken a cultural code, a religious rule or something. Perhaps they even thought he had stolen their souls. Anyway his pursuers were extremely angry whatever the cause. Fortunately, as so many were trying to follow him, they were getting in each other's way through the narrow allies and George was able to maintain a little distance between him and them. But, in the heat and dust, he was tiring; he couldn't keep going much longer. Suddenly he burst out of the narrow gut of the alley into the stomach of a small square. To his right was the mosque with people crowding in. Perhaps, if he could get in there he could lose himself in the throng. He dashed up the steps and slipped inside pushing rudely through and getting some angry looks as he settled into the rows of worshippers. He could hear his chasers still shouting as they neared the mosque, they must have seen him come in. God, was there no escape from this terror? He bowed his head in prayer, how could they find him among all these other people bowed in prayer?

Finally he could relax for a bit. For once his prayers had been answered and he had found a sanctuary, safe from whatever evil his pursuers wished to mete out on him.

Suddenly, he heard a shout from not far away and a disturbance clawed its way towards him through the masses. Ostrich like he buried his head down towards the floor but it was impossible; they seemed to be coming straight for him. He really did begin to pray now.

His hands were pressed to his face as he trembled, drenched with emotion, George was paralysed with terror and locked in panic.

A sharp tap on the sole of his shoe sent a shockwave through his body and he was able to turn his head and peer up behind him. A large man was towering over him, his arm raised and a cruel smile was twisting his face. So this was it, this was how it was all to end, tears flooded from his eyes as he thought of his wife, his widow. The giant of a man pushed his hand into George's face. He was holding a British passport.

THE LONG WALK

BY ROSEMARY SHEPPARD

She remembers that she was wearing her tan checked coat that day. Strange how certain things remain in the memory while others, more important, just evaporate. She can't recall how Martin was dressed – probably a tweed jacket and corduroy trousers and a jumper. It was late April and it was a chilly day, windy and raw. They had parked the car at the gates to the park and set off to walk. She doesn't think they had a particular destination in mind; they just needed to be away from other distractions so that they could talk it out though they both knew there was to be no way out of the situation they were in. Too much had already been said. So they strode along, the gulf between them as wide as the ocean and the mood equally blue.

She doesn't remember how the conversation began. She does remember that she felt consumed with sadness and despair. The disastrous previous weekend at the farm had probably been the worst she had ever spent and even now she can hardly bear to think back on it. The atmosphere between them had been wrong from the start and had just carried on getting worse, compounded by the presence of the small boy. She remembers clearly what an attractive boy he was: jet black hair and dark eyes and that knowing way about him, even though he could not have been more than about eight or nine years old.

The effect he had had on Martin had been daily more evident, raising doubts in her mind and yet she had never questioned Martin about it nor referred to the child at all, neither during the weekend nor during the long walk.

"I don't see how I can forget what you said to me," she murmured. "I want to but it's always going to be there." The tears began to flow. He'd told her, while they had been lying in bed together, that he'd felt absolutely nothing while they were making love. It was as though she had been struck by lightning. She had tried to be conciliatory, to suggest remedies, but he had been adamant. She had known then that there was to be no way back.

"It's not just that," Martin replied. "It's other things. I think I just said that to make a statement." He was starting to cry too. "I've never felt about anyone the way I felt about you."

She noticed the use of the past tense.

"Well then perhaps we can try and put that behind us and address the other things. There might be a way out of it." She was desperately trying to salvage their relationship. She wanted to marry him, have a family, be part of his family. She'd met them all and they had all taken to her. She saw the future she had been looking forward to suddenly being wrenched away from her.

"I don't think I can do that," he replied. She sensed that although he was obviously distressed, yet he was resolute. He had made up his mind and nothing she said was going to change it.

They walked and talked for – how long had it been? She thinks it must have been a couple of hours but it always came back to the same thing.

In the end she asked him, "What about the flat and all the arrangements?" The wedding was booked for three months' time and they had put the deposit down on the flat they had decided to buy.

"I'll get in touch with the solicitors and do the necessary." He was nothing if not practical, in spite of his tears.

Finally, through the blur of her own tears she watched herself take off the ring he had given her and hand it back to him.

"You'd better have this back." When he had told his family of their engagement, after what had indeed been a whirlwind romance, his mother had cross questioned them like a couple of naughty school children even though they were both in their late twenties. She had made a big fuss about Martin giving a family ring to a young woman he had known for such a short time, but that had all died down as the family had got to know her and, yes, taken her to their hearts. They were going to be very upset as would her own parents, not that her own mother had ever really cared much for Martin.

He took the ring and put it in his pocket.

"I know I'll never love anyone the way I've loved you," he said.

She remembers him driving her home and sensing the relief he felt when she got out of the car. She went indoors to her waiting mother and cried in her arms, talking it through for the rest of the afternoon and evening, totally lost and devastated.

In the days that followed it fell to her to break all the arrangements. Martin cut himself off completely from all that had gone before though he did pay the solicitor's bills. Occasionally, after that, they met at local functions and about a year later he rang to tell her that he was engaged to someone from the school where he worked. By that time, she knew that she was well rid of him and was well on the way to making a new life for herself.

Looking back she regards him with a total lack of feeling of any kind, but the memory of that long walk and the abject misery she had experienced that day will always remain with her.

Note: This story is the recently written true account of something which happened to me in 1977. The poem which follows is something I penned at the time.

A NASTY EXPERIENCE

BY ROSEMARY SHEPPARD

I've just had a nasty experience

Well, more of a dirty great knock.

When the man of your dreams

Isn't all that he seems

It comes as a bit of a shock

It started off slowly in January

And gathered momentum with speed

(But by April I knew

It was crazy, but true,

He'd rather just sit there and read!)

We went off to Athens on holiday.

The weather was sunny and fine.

When we'd shared a moussaka

And had a baklava

I really believed he was mine.

He asked me to marry him speedily.

I naturally said that I would.

Then he gave me a ring.

'T was a beautiful thing

And everything seemed as it should.

The news received wide acclamation

And the good wishes came thick and fast.

So a wedding was planned,

Plush enough, but not grand,

Some drinks and the usual repast.

I rang up the Registrar's Office

'T was on April the lst that I phoned.

Yes, I do think it's cruel.

It made me look a fool

'Cos I ended up being disowned.

The flat that we bought was quite lavish -

The bedroom was purple and white -

And the contract was signed

But you'd have to be blind

Not to see that things weren't going right.

We went down to Cornwall for Easter.

It wasn't a major success.

It's not funny to me

'Cos I got the big 'E'.

What a horrible, bloody great mess!

I had to break all the arrangements,

Though he paid the solicitor's bill.

If there's justice at all,

Be it ever so small,

He'll get his comeuppance. He will!!

ON LINE DATING

BY JOHN ROSS

There are times when things just don't work out and this was one of them.

Online dating. Never done it before and now decided that he never will again.

It was all because Charles and Debbie had said that he needed to get back out there, out into the dating market. He had been divorced for two years, not his fault, it was his ex-wife who had strayed. Maybe it was his fault that pushed her to it, but he still held the moral high ground.

It had been a rather drunken night at the Lion's Heart pub with Charles and Debbie when Debbie had said, "Why aren't you dating Tom? You're a good-looking man for your age. I am sure that there are plenty women out there who would jump through hoops to go out with you?"

"What, me? I'm forty-two, unfit, drink too much and really don't care." Tom was standing up finishing his pint of Ruddles County with one hand and trying to put on his jacket with the other. Charles helped him slip the sleeve onto his arm and then Debbie held the jacket for Tom to slip his other arm in when he put down the glass. "Look I am happy in my own space, I don't need a relationship."

Charles looked at him, "Tom my friend you need taken in hand, well if you know what I mean. You need to eat better, drink less beer and do some exercise. Being a forty something nowadays is almost like pushing thirty a few years ago, it's not time for the pipe and slippers yet."

That conversation had been six months ago, he was now pushing forty-three but he had joined a gym, enrolled in a cookery class to learn about how to cook well and live better and lost just under two stones in weight. Debbie had taken him shopping to buy a new wardrobe for casual as well as business and he now had some tight-fitting jeans, cool shirts, fashionable shoes as well as three new business suits with accompanying shirts and ties. In six months he had transformed himself into a new Tom. What he needed now was a new haircut.

Debbie again led the way, this time to the hairdresser. Not Tom's normal barber but some expensive, camp guy in a salon just off the High Street that was all loud music, mirrors, lights and expansive hand gestures.

"Julian, Tom needs something stylish, modern, cool, you know what I mean?" Debbie was looking at the back of Tom's head as he sat in the chair of the salon.

"Oh doesn't he just darling? ". Julian ran his fingers through Tom's hair, which Tom found a little annoying. "What have you been washing this with Tom? Fairy Liquid? It's in a terrible state." Before Tom could answer Debbie blew a kiss at him in the mirror and said, "I'll leave you with Julian, he is a marvel. I'll be back in about an hour. Got some shopping to do."

"An hour? Surely that's too long?" Tom was trying to stand and turn in the seat, Julian put one hand on Tom's shoulder and pushed him back down into the chair. He was stronger than he looked. "Just you sit there Tom and leave it all to me." The hand gestured outwards and the head look skywards as Julian summoned two of his minions to assist.

Shampoo, rinse, conditioner, leave to soak in, rinse, combed out, cut and styled like he had never been styled before. At the end of it all he had a shiny head of hair that was parted quite severely on the left and held in place with more product than he thought was healthy, but he looked good.

"Voila, the magic is done," Julian took half a step back his hands clutched to his chest as if he had just had some sort of religious revelation. Minion one started to sweep up the hair clippings, minion two offered him a coffee. He ordered an Americano and took a seat on the leather sofa in the waiting area, if he was honest he felt good about himself. He looked out of the window and an attractive looking woman in her thirties who was walking past, hesitated slightly to look at him through the glass, she smiled and walked on.

He was tapped on the shoulder by minion two with the coffee and then joined by Debbie who had sat next to him on the sofa, several high-quality paper bags with string handles and loud logos on them in her lap. "Looking good Tom, I told you he was a genius."

"Yeah well," Tom looked a little embarrassed as Julian was standing next to him holding out what looked like a book, which he took. As he opened it he realised it was the bill. This haircut had just cost him £85, he had never paid much more £12 before. The credit card took a hit before they both left and hit the street to make there way to Debbie's car.

"The transformation is now complete, we need to create your profile and get you on line Tom." They were driving towards Tom's flat.

"What do you mean 'profile'." He twisted in the passenger seat of the BMW Z4 to look at Debbie.

"You know, forty something, heterosexual male into sports, cooking, music, looking for attractive female to share experiences with, that sort of thing. Oh plus a couple of pictures."

"Effectively you are pimping me, that's what you're doing."

"Oh no darling never that, more a Pygmalion moment than a pimping one." She laughed, the creases at the sides of her eyes laughed with her, she really thought that this was funny.

At Tom's flat Debbie took some photographs, thoughtful ones, fun smiling ones and a smouldering one as she called it.

Debbie fired up her laptop and logged on to 'Singles Symmetry dot com', turned the laptop around and said, "Right mister, complete the form and the direct debit mandate, use the smouldering picture and the second fun one, off you go." With that she went off into the kitchen to make coffee for them both.

Tom completed the form, which he thought had to be a breach of personal information but did it anyway. At the bottom of the form he uploaded the two photographs and hit the post button. A message popped up thanking him for his post and that it would be reviewed prior to being uploaded onto the site, within the next 12 hours. "Done it now son," he said to himself, "no way back now, you are officially back in the game."

It was two days later when he received the e-mail from Singles Symmetry with the attachment. He hesitated before opening it. "Oh what the hell, in for a penny and all that." He mumbled to himself as he clicked on the file. The screen filled with a profile of a Mandy Richards, 33 years old, divorced, no children, blonde, blue eyed, 1m 63 cm tall. What the hell was that in feet and inches, he Googled it, just over 5 feet 4 inches. He was just under six feet so a bit of a difference but no problem. She was into going to concerts, reading, cooking and all kinds of exercise it said. Scrolling down he came to two photographs, one head and shoulders the other of her standing in a cream dress and shoes. She was easy on the eye, there was no doubt about that. At the very bottom of the page was a box to click on to arrange a meeting, he clicked it and it opened a form with three options of location, date and time. He filled them all in using three different restaurants for this coming Friday, Saturday and Sunday all at 8pm. Send.

About an hour later his mobile phone pinged indicating that he had an e-mail, he looked. It was from Mandy, confirming 8pm at Alfredo's on the Saturday. He had a date.

The few days in between flew by and it was now Saturday, he had booked the table, tried on a suit, discarded it, tried on the skinny jeans and discarded those also. As the weather was warm he opted for a pair of chinos, loafers, a polo shirt and draped a sweater around his shoulders. He had seen Italian men do this when he was on holiday and always thought it looked cool. A final look in the mirror and then waited for the taxi.

He arrived just before eight and was shown to the table, Mandy had not arrived yet. He ordered a glass of red wine and some still water and waited. At just after ten past eight Mandy made her entrance, and some entrance it was. She had opened the door of the restaurant but was still shouting at the taxi driver outside, "Bloody con man, that has to have been the longest route possible to get here you robbing bastard." The accent was a mix of East End and Essex with a hint of a nasal tone, it was not pleasant. The restaurant became very quiet as she turned her head inwards looking for a waiter or someone to show her to the table. "What!, ain't you never been ripped off before?" she exclaimed to anyone who would listen. Tom's mouth was wide open, what had he got himself into? "Hallo, yeah you, I'm here to meet Tom Andrews." A flustered waiter scurried over to take her coat and show her to Tom's table.

As she took off the lightweight coat her dress was revealed in all it's leopard skin glory and white stilettos. Tom stood as she walked over, the dress was like a second skin, but it was one size too small. The waiter pulled out the chair for her as the noise in the restaurant restarted, "Not bad in 'ere is it?" she said to Tom as she sat down, extending her hand across the table, he shook it, she looked disappointed as if she had expected him to kiss it.

As he looked at her face it hit him who she reminded him off, Marilyn Monroe, her hair was done in that style that she had in 'Some like it Hot' and her naivety was about the same.

Looking at Tom's glass she said to the waiter, "I'll 'ave one of those mate." The waiter scurried off.

"So Tom," she put on what she considered to be a sultry look which Tom thought made her look like she had wind, "I've read your profile an' that but I likes to hear it from the 'orses mowf like, so tell me about yourself while I 'ave a drink. I'm parched."

Tom was so astounded that he ran through his life story. Nice upbringing in Bedfordshire, University, moved to London with his job, met Caroline and got married, got divorced twelve years later, no kids and his friends had told him to get back into the dating game.

"All very nice 'an that Tom, but where are you livin' right now? Where's that waiter need anuver drink." She looked round and waved the empty glass in the air with her leopard skin clad arm. The waiter lifted a bottle and walked over.

"I live in Blackheath, close to Vanburgh Park, do you know the area?" he asked, not knowing why he asked, just being polite.

"Nah, sowf of the river innit, don't go sowf of the river me, Ilford, Seven Kings, that's me patch." The waiter had refilled both glasses and was waiting to take the food order.

"I'll have the mushrooms and the steak, rare," Mandy did not look up at the waiter as she ordered. "and sir?"

"I'll have the prawns and the steak, medium to well please, with the dauphinoise potatoes," he was just handing the menu back to the waiter when Mandy said, "What sort of spuds?"

"Dauphinoise, they are sliced thin, cooked in cream and garlic, very tasty." He explained.

"Nah, not for me that Frog muck, I'll have chips wiv mine." The waiter sniffed the air in disgust as he walked away.

"It's nice in 'ere, bit far mind from Ilford. Do you use this gaff often then?" She was looking at him across the table and twiddling with the blonde curl on the left side of her head.

As he made to reply he swore that her hair moved slightly. Ignoring it he said that he worked nearby and had used this particular restaurant several times, "Oh so they know you then? That'll be how he brought me straight over."

Tom considered that he would probably never set foot in this restaurant again as Mandy continued twiddling her hair. It definitely moved, it had to be a wig. Should he tell her or not? Too late. Her twiddling had pulled the wig to one side and as she sneezed it came off in her hand revealing a hair net and streaked black rooted hay coloured hair underneath. Mandy looked at the wig in her left hand as she wiped her nose with her right hand, sniffing as she said, "That's a bit embarrassing innit? I think it best of I make me exit don't you? Gimme a call and we can do this properly some uvver time." She stood up and tried to reposition the wig as she walked towards the door.

The relieved waiter was there with her coat which he helped her put on as she was part way through the entrance, "Good night madam." He said as he turned to look at Tom sitting with two glasses of red wine in front of him. One of which he picked up and gulped down.

"Would you like me to cancel the order sir?" asked the waiter

"I think that might be prudent Georgio. Thank you, just the cheque for the drinks if you don't mind?"

"Sir, as frequent customer whose patronage we value, I think that you have had a very lucky escape and I think we should toast to that. The drinks are on us, have a good evening."

Georgio walked behind the bar counter and Tom drank the other glass, painfully aware of the eyes starting at him from several tables.

"On line dating," he thought to himself, "never again."

FLASH

BY OWEN SUTHERLAND

Flash – scorched dots jangle

Triangular circles smell of noses

A pocket watch slithers – seconds frozen

Tumbling toes tangle cotton socks

Flat screen spots perspective puzzles

Jostling snowdrops blow crimson bubbles

Inflated mushrooms beating war drums

An aching rainbow tied in knots

Shredded shadows drip to shapeless clots

Beneath the splintered sticks of cultured box.

Smiling laughter spirals sideways

Gurgling grunting gone to waste

Sizzling squeaks of sense evaporated

Acid base of human race vaporised

Condescending drips of nucleotides

Strung along a clothes line in the sun

Recycled atoms of a star back where all begun

A new race a different tumble in the uv ray

Just enjoy this time – this moment – our day.

Note: This was partly written on a ferry, Bilbao to Portsmouth when we heard about the North Korea nuclear bomb tests.

Our writing topic encouraged me to try a more surreal approach to which the mutually assured destruction of our nuclear age – bought to prominence by North Korea's bomb testing – seemed well fitted.

Let's hope our lucky escape continues.

THE RUNAWAY

BY DOT GARRETT

Scott stood on the platform and stared down the line. "The next train should be in very shortly," the man at the ticket booth had said.

"Please let it come soon," he silently pleaded as he rearranged his rucksack on his shoulders. It felt heavy already. He felt like he had the weight of the world on his shoulders but it wasn't just his personal belongings that weighed heavily; he had just made the biggest decision of his life and there was no going back.

He shivered as the reality hit him hard and the fear of the unknown crowded into his thoughts. He pulled himself together; nothing could possibly be as bad as being at home. He had an adventure ahead of him and the streets might not be paved in gold in the big city but he would give it his best shot. Scott knew he had only himself to rely on now.

Finally, the train pulled into the station and Scott settled into a seat near the window. As he stared out at the countryside rushing by he thought of his mum and the life he had just left behind. He desperately hoped that she would be alright but he also knew that nothing he could do would change anything.

Barry, his mum's boyfriend, had moved in with them four years ago when Scott was ten. The fighting and arguing had started almost straight away. Scott would lie in his bed listening to his mum's screams and the thuds of Barry hitting her. He was so scared he would cry and pray for it to stop.

The next day Scott's mum would cuddle him after Barry went to work but Scott could feel her flinch as he hugged her back. "Make him go, please Mum!" pleaded Scott, but his mum would shake her head.

The last couple of years, Scott had been planning his escape. Barry had lashed out at him many times as Scott grew bigger and, although his mum begged Barry not to, she always got a beating for trying to protect him. "It would be best if I just go," thought Scott.

He had saved as much pocket money as he could and earned some more by doing odd jobs for the neighbours such as cleaning their cars and sweeping up leaves. He had over two hundred pounds saved when, on the previous Friday; Barry had beaten his mum so badly she had been taken to hospital; not for the first time. Scott knew he couldn't be at home when Barry came back; he knew Barry would take it out on him and hit him when his mum was not there.

Scott had made a quick search of the house and found another forty pounds to add to his savings. He had stuffed as many of his clothes as he could into his school rucksack and decided to put his plan into action. It wasn't much of a plan but he knew, if he got away and made it to London, he was willing to work and he guessed he could pass for sixteen; it would be his fifteenth birthday next month after all.

As the train pulled into Euston station Scott initially felt overwhelmed by so many people rushing everywhere. He decided to get a burger and coke and then check out where he could stay.

As he sat at the burger bar he was surprised when a smartly dressed woman with a young boy, who looked about twelve or thirteen, approached him.

"Are you on your own, dear?" she asked Scott and he hesitated, unsure what to reveal. "Oh sorry, I didn't mean to frighten you," she added, "only I wondered if George could sit with you while I go and get our meal."

"Yeah, sure he can" replied Scott, visibly relaxing.

"Is that your mum?" Scott asked George.

"No, um, my aunty" said George as he looked down.

"She looks a bit like my mum," said Scott, with a sigh "although my mum has got brown hair not blonde."

When the woman came back with their food she asked Scott lots of questions; where he lived, what was he doing in London on his own, where was he staying. She smiled a lot and kept hugging George and telling him he was her favourite nephew.

Scott was reluctant to tell her about his home life but when she went to the counter again and came back with brownies for them all he found himself blurting out his unhappiness.

"Oh you poor lamb," she said. "I think it is fate that brought us together today and you must let me help you."

Oh, no, I don't want to trouble you," said Scott

"Call me Aunt Jane," said the woman "and he can come back with us, George, can't he, just until he finds a job," she added.

George looked down again and just shrugged.

As the three of them left the station and made their way through the busy streets Scott felt glad that he had made a friend so quickly.

After walking about twenty minutes they turned into a side street with lots of tall houses and Aunt Jane let them into one about halfway down the street. The sounds of the traffic had receded and it felt quite peaceful away from all the hustle and bustle of the busy, London high-street.

"Come on in," said Aunt Jane and Scott noticed that George hung back. "We are on the third floor," she added as they climbed the steep staircase.

Aunt Jane showed Scott a neat bedroom with just a cupboard and a high window with matching curtains and bedcover.

"Put your bag down and come and find us in the kitchen. I will make some hot chocolate for us all," said Aunt Jane.

Scott took some of his clothes from his bag and then looked for the bathroom before finding Aunt Jane and George in the kitchen.

"Here you are, drink this, you must be tired and want to rest," Aunt Jane said as she handed Scott a mug of hot chocolate.

Scott felt his eyes starting to close before he had finished his drink.

He woke up and his head was hurting. He didn't know where he was at first and then realised he was in the bed at Aunt Jane's house. He was surprised to find he had no clothes on. He struggled to stand and then searched around for his clothes. His bag was missing and the few things he had put in the cupboard were gone. He wrapped the bedcover around himself and tried the door. It was locked. He pulled the curtain back and realised that the high window was barred. Fear prickled over his skin. What had he done?

Just then he heard the key turn in the lock. Expecting it to be Aunt Jane he shouted "Where is my stuff?"

To Scott's surprise a man walked into the room.

"Who are you? Where is Aunt Jane?"

The man was tall, with dark hair and a moustache; he was wearing a smart suit. He locked the door behind him, putting the key into his pocket. He sat down and patting the bed beside him he said "Come and sit here, Scott. You can call me Uncle Joe and we are going to be good friends if you just do as you're told."

It was three months later before Scott could try to make his escape. Finally, as the weather got colder, he was allowed a tracksuit to wear when he wasn't entertaining Uncle Joe and his friends. He knew now that they put drugs into his drinks to make him more compliant but he had never known such pain.

Uncle Joe had just brought in his breakfast and, when he'd left the bedroom, Scott realised he hadn't heard the key turn in the lock. He waited a few minutes and then tried the door. It opened. Scott furtively looked down the hall and could hear the faint sound of voices coming from the kitchen. Silently, he made for the main door and this opened too. He couldn't believe his luck. Scott crept down the stairs and, finally, he was there, at the street door. He opened it and staggered out. He had no shoes but he didn't care. Taking big gulps of air, he made his way quickly to the end of the street where he joined the hustle and bustle of the crowds going about their daily business. No one looked at Scott and his bare feet as he went with the flow.

Very soon he realised he was back where he started, at Euston station. With his head down he wondered what to do now. He couldn't believe his luck when he saw a pound coin on the ground. Picking it up, he made up his mind to phone his mum, the only person he wanted to talk to. He found the phone boxes and, going to the one at the end, he dialled his home number.

His mum answered "Hello" and, after a few seconds, "Who is there?"

For a few moments Scott was lost for words, he was so overwhelmed to hear his mum's voice again. "It's me, Mum, Scott"

"Oh Scott, darling, I'm so pleased to hear from you. I've been searching everywhere for you. I thought I'd lost you," cried his Mum. "Where are you?"

"I'm in London, but, Mum, can I come home please? Will Barry be cross with me?"

"Listen, Scott! When I was in hospital the nurses and social worker persuaded me to finally press charges against Barry. I have got a protection order now and he can't come near us," she sobbed, adding "but I thought I was too late. I thought I'd lost you Scott. Please forgive me for being so weak before. Just come home now!"

Scott was overwhelmed with relief but then he explained to his mum that he didn't have any money and some bad people might be looking for him.

"I think my money will run out now," he added. "I am at Euston train station."

"Listen, Scott", said his mum. "You must find a policeman and tell him I am coming on the next train".

As his money ran out he could hear his mum saying "I love you Scott..."

Scott stepped out from the phone box and, as he looked around, he suddenly saw Aunt Jane across the concourse, speaking into her mobile phone and heading straight towards him. He turned in the opposite direction and ran as fast as he could but tripped on someone's wheelie bag. As strong hands helped him up, he looked into the welcome face of a policeman.

"What's your rush, sonny?"

Scott wildly looked around but there was no sign of Aunt Jane. As he looked at the policeman, a fat tear started down his face and he finally felt safe.

Note: In a previous life I worked with abused children, as I wrote the story it took on a life of its own and I was so glad that Scott found his way home. Unfortunately many don't. With grateful thanks to NSPCC; Womens Aid and Barnardo's charities.

NO REGRETS

BY CAROLYN SIMS

"And now the end is near

And so I face the final curtain."

Well, my dear, you do face the final curtain. Those dark red, velvet drapes will soon part as you sail off silently into the sunset. How often did you say that about your cronies who 'popped their clogs' as you so delicately put it. "The only things sure in life are death and taxes," another of your misquoted witticisms you shared with your coterie of golf buddies, whilst dissecting the round of golf you had just played. Did you play for pleasure or for one-upmanship?

I did not mind your Sunday mornings at the course, or the two hours at the bar socialising, or was it 'networking', the expression you frequently used to excuse your absence at home.

"My friend, I'll say it clear,

I'll state my case of which I'm certain.

I lived a life that's full.."

Yes, Keith, this is the hymn you chose to follow Onward Christian Soldiers and I vow to thee my country. I thought it in very poor taste, but the vicar told me lots of people think it appropriate for funerals. You did live a full life, but not necessarily with me, of course, but maybe you did not notice. The golf club, Rotary, the Town Council and Masons all featured in your life, but not me, apart from the dinner dances, Ladies' night and Christmas dos.

"I travelled each and every highway

And more, much more than this,

I did it my way."

You know, you were right. This is a good choice for a final hymn for you. We did travel a lot in later years, but how much did you actually see? Every holiday was like an American tour; "If it's Tuesday it must be Naples". We never had time to appreciate anything. Art bored you. The Sistine Chapel only aroused your warped sense of humour. "How did the bugger lie on his back to paint that?" Walking was for those who could not drive. The lovely evening gondola ride was spoilt by you singing "Just one Cornetto". I could have died with embarrassment, who cares if it was sung to the Queen Mother? Then there was swimming. It had to be in a pool because of the pollution in the sea. We never stood and just soaked up the view. I think we sat on more bar stools than sun loungers, and if I spoke to someone you did not approve of – they were too posh, academic, gay or a person of colour, I had the humiliation of having to snub them later. It was too painful to bear to see the confusion in their eyes.

"Regrets, I had a few

But then again, too few to mention.

I did what I had to do, and saw it through without exemption."

Yes, you were certainly very successful, but regrets I doubt it. You never had a sleepless night worrying about some deal you had finalised, or had second thoughts about cutting staff at the factory.

"And more, much more than this

I did it my way."

Even on the council democracy was an unknown word to you, let alone concept. Bluster, bullying and conflict got you what you wanted. The building projects for houses and schools were all very commendable but it was no accident who got the contacts - you and your pals. "Stick together lads there's strength in numbers", another of your little quips.

"Yes, there were times, I'm sure you knew

When I bit off more than I could chew."

No, I did not know. I never knew. You didn't share your life with me. You were a wonderful provider, but it was your mortgage, your house, the holiday was chosen and booked by one of your female lackeys. I just went along as the 'little woman' who was required to dress up 'nice', hair and nails immaculate and three inch heels to set off the outfit. I was the good wife – excellent cook, passable housewife, but then Mrs. Dobbs did most of the cleaning twice a week. The house keeping account was generous, as was the dress allowance, but did you ever say you liked the dinner party fare, or the slinky black numbers I starved myself to wear, and then endure the jokey comments "she scrubs up well." Yes, you lapped up the congratulatory comments about me, as if I was the new car or the 'smart' TV.

"I've lived, I laughed and cried

I've had my fill, my share of losing

And now...."

And now it's about me. After forty four years I have had my fill, my share of losing a life that had so much promise. You were a good looking bloke in the 1960s, fun to be with and full of dreams for the future. You said that you picked me out at the Roxy; I was the best looking girl on the dance floor. We made plans, I thought it would be a future we would share, build together as equal partners. Maybe I was too easily manipulated, too trusting and too keen to show my love by not voicing my opinions. I did not want you to think that I was disloyal or conflicting. Then, as the years went by, no children came along to give me a role and you seemed to find your life outside the home and not with me.

"And may I say, not in a shy way.

Oh no, oh no not me. I did it my way."

Now it's my turn to do it my way. After the champagne and finger buffet I shall let myself go. No more crippling patent leather shoes and tight cocktail dresses. They are already bundled up in a couple of black plastic sacks awaiting delivery to the Oxfam shop in the town centre. I shall never eat another lettuce leaf or drink slimline tonic. Tomorrow I am going on a spending spree at M & S. Elasticated trousers and nice comfy woollies are on the shopping list.

The house is already up for sale and a cute little bungalow with a lovely garden has just come on the market. You didn't know I liked gardening did you? You just presumed that Bert Wilson did all the planting out and pruning but we kept our little secret, he cut the lawns and trimmed the edges. I was well satisfied and he was well paid.

Yes, I know, I said bungalow. You always said you wouldn't be seen dead in a bungalow but you are dead, dear, so you can't veto my plans. I have booked a Mediterranean cruise with the Princess line for September. I plan to talk to anyone who appears interesting and thinks I am interesting too. So, thank you, my dear, I shall try not to have any regrets and take a leaf out of your book and do it my way.

THE BLIND DATE

BY JENNIFER NESTEROFF

Katelin crept into the restaurant and hid behind a pillar which was situated near the main entrance. From there she had a clear view of the dining area. She searched the room for a man sitting at a table on his own. There were four of these and she decided she didn't care for the looks of any of them.

"Why on earth did I agree to have dinner with some bloke I've never seen, again? God, I must be lonely!"

She had finally said she would do this as a favour for a colleague, David, at work who was desperately searching for someone to take this person off his hands so that he could accept an invitation to a party from an absolute dish he had just met. David's mother had made him promise to look after the son of a friend of her friend who would be coming to the city for the first time.

"So, what's he like, this son of a friend of a friend?" Katelin asked.

"Don't know, never met him but he's probably all right," said David, brightly, while giving her a dog – like pleading look. "Who knows? He might even turn out to be the man of your dreams!"

"Oh, sure, and pigs might fly." Katelin had had her fill of blind dates.

After the break-up with the proverbial 'love of her life', Katelin had, at first, sworn off men forever but after many nights of sitting alone at home with the cat, she finally decided to give it all another try and joined the world of hopeful blind-daters. It did not go well!

Her first date had turned out to be a member of an alternative religious group who was collecting wives.

This was followed by a series of woeful disappointments.

The final discouragement came when she had dated someone who confided in her that he was secretly from another planet and would love to whisk her away to his love nest in the heavens where she would be treated like a queen by all his double-headed, furry faced friends. Just as they were ordering desserts, this fascinating man was approached by two officers in uniform who, after apologising to Katelin, whisked him away, hopefully to a more earthly abode with locks on the doors. Katelin was not sorry. After that experience, it was not surprising that she lost heart and decided that blind-dating did not hold any promise for her and that she would simply resign herself to leading a solitary life.

Now she had let herself in for another probable disaster.

Just then, a waiter noticed her as she took another quick peek and asked her if she would like to come in.

"No, I'm still deciding," whispered Katelin. "Please go away."

"Well, we have a delicious and varied cuisine and I'm sure you could find something that would appeal to you if you would care to take the chance."

"I'm not worried about the food. It's the man that's the problem."

"Pardon?"

Katelin sighed, "Look, I'm supposed to meet a man I don't know for dinner here. I think he must be one of the four I can see and I'm not too sure I would care for any of them. Oh, wait, it's only three now. The fat one's wife has just come back from the powder-room."

The waiter, whose name was Giovanni, had a kind heart and a Southern European inclination to help ladies in distress, especially pretty ones. He glanced around the room.

"No, it's still four; I think you have missed Mr. Simms in the corner. He is one of our regulars but being 92 I rather doubt that he's your man."

"Oh, I wouldn't be surprised," muttered Katelin, "but no, this one has a mother, which I don't think your Mr. Simms would have at this point."

"Why don't you go out with men you know? That way it would all be less of a mystery," wondered Giovanni.

"Well, I haven't been able to find a decent man since the one I wanted did a bunk, the bastard, so I did a bit of blind-dating which was unbelievable. How many creeps are out there? Now I am just doing someone a favour."

"Well, if you like, I can ask at the reception desk if any of the men in the room is waiting to meet a young lady."

"Yes, that would be helpful"

Giovanni went to the desk and came back, looking pleased.

"Our receptionist has received a message for you from someone called David to say that your date can't make it tonight. His plane was cancelled. She has been looking out for you but, not surprisingly, she didn't think to look behind this pillar."

"Oh well, I can go home then."

"Er, I was thinking perhaps you might consider having dinner after all with someone you have met this time."

"And who would that be?"

"Well, me actually, I am just finishing my shift here and I could be ready in ten minutes."

For the first time Katelin really looked at Giovanni. He was tall and well-built and she noticed that his bright blue eyes were really rather startling. Besides that and most importantly, he seemed quite normal and nice.

"I think I would like that," she smiled.

Giovanni smiled back "Right then, I won't be long and then I'll take you to a decent restaurant. The food in this place is awful."

JAM AND JERUSALEM

BY ROSEMARY SHEPPARD

A number of years ago my husband and I found ourselves living in a small village in darkest Somerset and being of a friendly and helpful disposition, in other words, at a total loss to know how to fill my days while my husband was at work, I decided to join the Women's Institute – you know, the Jam and Jerusalem brigade. Those who remembered me in my younger, carefree, days when I lived and worked in London might have found it hard to think of me as one of that stalwart group of mainly gentrified ladies traditionally seen in pearls and twin-sets who produce jars of marmalade and pickles not to mention the aforesaid jam together with fairy cakes and knitted matinee jackets for fairs and bazaars, decorate the local church on high days and holidays and generally do good works among the poor and needy but I plunged in with both hands and found I really enjoyed it.

I hadn't been a member for very long when our first Christmas in the village loomed and I was asked if I would help to organise the annual festive meal to which all those who were, shall we say, not among the white collar brigade, were invited as a sort of thank you for their help during the year.

This would take place in the village hall, during the evening of the 21st December the menu to consist of a hearty soup with home-baked bread, turkey with all the trimmings, roast and boiled potatoes and a variety of vegetables, followed by good old Christmas Pudding accompanied by custard and brandy butter.

This all sounded very straightforward and ordinary to me and nothing to get very excited about until one of my fellow members let it slip that guests would be greeted on their arrival with a glass of heavily fortified mulled wine before being invited to take their seats for the meal, and that the brandy butter was a speciality of our Chairperson, Peggy Wood, whose hand was known to linger very lovingly with the brandy when she made it. In fact it was rumoured that many people came along just for that alone. Wine would also flow very freely throughout the evening and a good time would be had by all. If past years were anything to go by, most people would be barely able to stagger home at the end of the evening but as the 21st was to be a Saturday, they would not have to worry about getting up early the next morning to go about their business, all that is except for the farmers. However it was thought that as they were often used to having their nights disturbed by things like lambing etc. and never seemed to care about losing a bit of sleep particularly if free booze was involved they wouldn't worry about it.

I began to wonder what I was letting myself in for.

Apart from being asked to join in the making of the Christmas Puddings, I was given the job of contacting all the prospective guests, and asking for their confirmation that they would be coming along on the night. Once again this all seemed quite straightforward and I was provided with the list from the previous year which hadn't deviated much from any of the years before it. I was told, however, that there were a couple of people on this list who felt that it was totally beneath them to accept charity from the knobs of the village, as they put it, and wouldn't have been seen dead at the do, but who would equally have been exceedingly put out if they had not received the customary invitation. Everyone else, it seemed, was positively looking forward to what was, I was reliably informed by Mabel, my lady what does, 'the event of the season in these 'ere parts'.

Invitations were duly distributed and no refusals were forthcoming, apart from the ones we had anticipated. Arrangements went ahead accordingly.

As the 21st December drew closer I found myself being increasingly drawn into the spirit of the occasion. Having casually asked Mabel one day what she intended to wear I was more than a little surprised to hear that she and her best friend, Heather, who ran the general store cum post office in the village, had taken themselves off to the nearest big town the previous week and each treated themselves to a suitable gown for the evening. Their husbands would be attired in their best suits with new ties. Accustomed as I was to the more cosmopolitan existence of city life and still not fully understanding of the workings of a small village, this shook me rather. In fact I found myself utterly dumbfounded that a simple meal in a local village hall should evoke such enthusiasm, but it seemed that Mabel's epithet of it being the event of the season had been truly spoken.

During the two weeks leading up to the 21st the anticipation continued to grow and no-one I met could talk of anything but the meal.

Having been born and brought up in Surrey, I sometimes found it a trifle difficult to cope with the Somerset dialect, but I was working on it. However the excitement engendered by the forthcoming social function confounded all my efforts and trying to converse with the locals when they had almost reached a fever pitch of enthusiasm had the effect of making me feel like a foreigner, which, of course, I was.

Anyway, the plans for the evening of the 21st were drawn up and we ladies were called to a meeting by Peggy to be given our instructions. She had even gone to the trouble of writing everything down so that there would be no misunderstanding and handed us each a copy as she went through the details.

1. Ladies will wear black, with white aprons. The tables will have been decorated during the afternoon and there will be a Christmas Cracker at each place.

2. When guests arrive they will be handed a glass of mulled wine, which can be topped up on request. There will to be no self service. (This was underlined) This will preclude any unseemly rushing and grabbing.

3. Guests will then be seated according to a table plan which will be pinned up at the entrance and which will preclude any unseemly rushing and grabbing, saving of chairs for friends etc. etc.

4. Guests will be served their meals at their seats, silver service style. We will distribute a bread roll to every side plate. In that way there will be no unseemly rushing and grabbing etc. etc. Butter will already be on the table. We will then go round and ladle soup into everyone's bowl. Once this has been eaten we will clear away.

5. Guests will then receive a plate bearing a generous portion of turkey with sage and onion stuffing, sausage and bacon rolls, and then we will follow up with trays of vegetables which we will serve to each person. In that way there will be no unseemly rushing and grabbing, no-one hogging all the roast potatoes to the detriment of the slowest etc. etc. Once this has been eaten we will once more clear away.

6. Finally, the lights will be lowered, the Christmas Puddings will be doused in brandy and lit and carried into the room while everyone sings "We wish you a Merry Christmas!", with the accent on the lines "Now bring us some Figgy Pudding!". The puddings will be served and jugs of custard will be placed on the table along with large bowls of brandy butter. (At this point my friend whispered to me that if I'd never seen unseemly rushing and grabbing on a grand scale before, then that would be the moment.)

7. Throughout the meal members' husbands, dressed in dinner suits, will be passing among the tables refilling wine glasses in a fairly abstemious manner.

8. Once the pudding has been eaten the plates will be cleared and mince pies will be served with coffee or tea.

Right, everyone knew what they had to do. Were there any questions?

There was a deathly hush but one of our members was obviously intent on making her views felt for as if from nowhere a paper aeroplane clearly fashioned from the list of instructions suddenly launched into the air and slowly made its way round the hall while we sat and watched it. It was all I could do not to laugh out loud and I could hear giggling coming from all around me. Eventually, after several tours of the hall and as if by magic it came to ground right next to Peggy who had studiously ignored it throughout and who carried on.

"Ladies!" she cried, "I am relying on you all to make the evening a success. Let battle commence!"

It really did sound like some sort of military campaign. I relayed the events of the afternoon to my husband and we simply fell about laughing. It could almost have been the script for some sort of a Carry on Film. After all, we were only going to be serving dinner to ordinary country folk in a village hall. How difficult could it be! How wrong could we be!

When I look back upon that evening, most of it, happily, blurs into some sort of melee of noise and perpetual motion. From the moment the doors opened and the first of the guests entered the hall, it was utter pandemonium. The mulled wine ran out three times and in the end Peggy had to stand on a chair and call for order at which point some bright spark called out "we'll have three more pints please, when you're ready".

Finally we managed to get everyone seated, not necessarily where they were supposed to be sitting according to the plan and by this time the soup was really past its best but nobody seemed to care. I can't remember who it was who threw the first bread roll but in the ensuing fracas little Doris Crampton got hit on the head by one poorly aimed shot and amazed everyone by the language which she came out with, not at all the sort of thing you expect from someone of nearly ninety.

By the time the soup had been cleared away, I was beginning to feel exhausted but the worst was yet to come. Silver service has such a lovely ring about it but this was nothing like what happened in the village hall. There I stood behind Bob Simmons, platter laden with roast potatoes in one hand and spoon and fork in the other, all ready to dispense my goodies when he simply grabbed the tray out of my hands and shovelled the best part of the contents onto his plate, while I stood there just looking on. Happily, the ladies who were slaving away in the kitchen were old hats at the situation and had spares for such occurrences and we managed to give everyone what they wanted.

At one point I managed to ask my friend as we rushed past each other in the kitchen gathering top ups for our empty platters whether it was always like this and she just nodded and raised her eyebrows with a pained expression.

After that, as I said, most of it became a blur - however I do seem to remember everyone singing the Figgy Pudding song in a very spirited manner which would have done Wembley Stadium proud. We had been unable to light the puddings because someone had drunk the brandy but it didn't seem to matter. Everyone was well and truly lit up themselves by then.

By the time the last guest finally went home – at about four o'clock the next morning – most of the men legless and a lot of the women too, I was completely exhausted, not to mention a gibbering wreck.

My husband wandered over to where I had collapsed into a chair and offered me a tipple from his cunningly concealed flask.

"Well done, old girl", he said.

"Bloody hell!" I said, "I think we were lucky to escape with our lives." I drank deeply and thought for a minute.

"Do you know the moment that will sum it all up for me?" I said, finally. "It's something someone said while I was attempting to serve the vegetables. It was that awful chap who runs the cycle repair place with the twitty wife who never speaks. As I bent over him with my platter in my hand, he looked up at me, his paper hat over one eye, said he'd have carrots and peas and then indicating his wife, uttered that immortal line 'but 'er, me - no parsnips'!!!"

Note: As a member of our Creative Writing Group, I am accustomed to writing a story in line with the phrase or word which is given to us at the meetings as a theme for or to be included in our next piece of work. One week the phrase we were presented with was 'butter me no parsnips', not something which immediately brings a story to mind. Anyway, I gave it some thought and came up with the above – purely fictitious, I'm afraid. I hope you enjoy it.

SHADOW WORLD

BY VONNIE GILES

"Wake up, you dozy mare! Looking for an early grave, are you?" shouted the coachman as the horses bore down upon her. It was only by a whim of destiny, that she was not trampled to death, then and there, in the middle of a Parisian thoroughfare; which in hindsight might have been a blessing in disguise! Perhaps a lucky escape, perhaps not! Certainly nothing good came from what followed – not until the very end, that is!

The clopping of the horses' hooves; the clatter of the carriage wheels; the slippery, wet, glistening cobbles under her feet; the jostling, the pushing, the sharp elbows, the jabbing umbrellas, the raucous shouts of the vendors –everything, everything was so palpably jagged and painful that she could surely cut her fingers on it as if it were a knife. Marguerite wanted to shout out loud for it all to stop, for the ceaseless hurly-burly to end, but the words wouldn't leave her lips! How the shop girls, the tradesmen, the delivery boys would have stared at this seemingly mad woman if she had!

Where was the comfort and the ease that a few drops of laudanum would have brought her? Where were the dreams that protected her from reality? How she longed to be once more in her shadowy, cotton-wool world where she always felt safe! What wouldn't she have given at that moment for her tincture of opium, for her calming glass of absinthe glowing like liquid emeralds!

However, fate had something different in store for her; a little tableau had miraculously, wondrously suddenly appeared in front of her eyes. Her nemesis had returned and now that she had finally found him again, she had no time for such indulgences, however strong her craving for drink and drugs might be.

"My darling girl, my angel in blue, how I love you, how I want you! My beautiful Veronique!" she heard him say. Plump, smug, elegantly dressed, he was holding an umbrella over a lovely girl in a brilliant, frilled and furbelowed blue dress who was about to enter his carriage.

Of course, it was always like that at the start of the affaire. The girl, young, pretty, fresh-faced, innocent of the ways of the world, flattered that a man obviously so rich and well-born should be attracted to her! All those years ago, she too had been like that, she too had wanted him; she too had even thought herself in love with him.

"But, believe me, little girl in blue," she thought, "he's not worth loving, as you will soon find out. I wonder where he found you – serving in a shop, working below stairs in a friend's house? However, one day soon, you will give anything to be back selling pretty baubles to the gentry, to be cleaning out the grate at six o'clock on a freezing, cold morning, your hands covered in ash!"

As Marguerite, half-fascinated, watched the little scene, the tall, imposing buildings of the city seemed to close around her and she, once again, withdrew within herself; for some odd reason, the only thing of which she was now conscious was the moisture seeping through the soles of her thin shoes. She knew, however, that painful as it might be, she had to reach out to the harsh world if she were to have any contact with him! For speak to him she must! The poor girl in her gorgeous, blue dress must escape his clutches. So gathering up her courage, she walked towards him, aware of how shabby, how careworn she must look!

"Augustine! Augustine!" she shouted at him; and as he heard his name, recognising her voice even after all these years, he almost threw the vision in blue into the carriage. He gave Marguerite a look of total disbelief and dismay, for she, of all the women whom he had used and abused, was the one whom he least wanted to see again.

She raised her voice so that she might be heard above the noises of the street.

"Surprised to see me, are you, Augustine? Thought me dead, did you, Augustine? Have you never wondered what happened to me, Augustine?"

"Go away, Marguerite! Your day has long gone! Keep your voice down!"

The wide eyes of the girl in blue stared out at her from the carriage window and the horses stirred restlessly, eager to be on their way.

"You're the devil incarnate, Augustine! I was as pure as the driven snow when I met you and well you know it! And just in case you should ever wonder, your daughter was born dead; as much a victim as I, of the opium and absinthe with which you plied me. Scarlet poppies and the green enchantress – they were our downfall! How long before that poor girl you've got there is another victim?"

At these words, Augustine stepped abruptly into the carriage and, tapping his umbrella on the floor, signalled for the coachman to move away. Veronique, trembling turned her pale, anxious face towards him, her eyes brimming with tears.

"Who was that woman, Augustine? So lovely, but so distraught! I felt so sorry for her!"

"A mad woman, my dear! One meets them, I'm afraid, when one ventures into the streets of Paris."

"She knew you, Augustine! She called you by your name! What was she talking about? What's absinthe?"

"Believe me, it's …it's all a nothingness, not something that you should worry your pretty, little head about. Come, Veronique, forget that it happened and let's enjoy the rest of the afternoon, shall we? However, perhaps, if you're a really good girl I even might introduce you to the pleasures of absinthe and you'll soon wonder how you could ever have lived without it!"

He took her gloved hand and kissed it.

Marguerite watched as the carriage disappeared into the mêlée of traffic and, now, desperate to return to her shadow world, she walked briskly a short distance up the street, until fate once more intervened, and she chose a brightly-decorated café where she seated herself at a table outside on the pavement. There she sat under the red, white and blue awning, sheltering from the lightly-falling rain.

An elderly waiter, destiny's messenger, in his long, white apron, came out to serve her, eyeing her shabby clothes curiously, yet noticing, at the same time, the voice and manners of a lady. She gave him her order and, within a few minutes, the sharp edges of her existence were once again softening and blurring. Then the waiter spoke the words that were to seal her fate.

"Madame, forgive my impertinence, but do you know the gentleman to whom you were speaking? I ask, because, believe me, he is someone whom you should avoid at all cost."

Marguerite extracted a bottle of laudanum from her pocket and added some of the liquid to her absinthe.

"That poor girl in the blue dress!" he continued. "She now thinks that she is on her way to have a romantic walk by the Seine and then to hear mass in Notre Dame, but as evening approaches and darkness falls he will push her against a wall and all her self respect will have gone forever; the down-and-outs and the derelicts who inhabit the river banks can vouch for my words. It would appear that this is how he prefers to arrange things – not for him a luxurious apartment, a discreet hotel! I hope Madame will forgive me for speaking so bluntly."

Marguerite had desperately wanted to shut out the sound of his words, but she, nevertheless, thanked him for his kindness, letting her thoughts slip and slide hazily over what he had said. Very soon, the innocent girl in blue, the latest victim of this foul man's desires, was going to find herself disgraced and disowned, a fallen woman, with no option but to walk the streets of Paris – as Marguerite had done before her!

She ordered another glass of absinthe and again added a few drops of laudanum. The mixture gleamed and glittered as the café lights were turned on to combat the early evening gloom. There she sat for another ten minutes, then rose and walked unsteadily and slowly along the street, now no longer perturbed by the hustle and bustle of the crowds or by the traffic, knowing exactly where she was going.

Thank goodness the rain, for the moment at least, had ceased to fall as she silently made her way down the flight of steps that led to the river-side, where in the distance, through the dimness, she could just make out two unmistakable figures; and hear their laughter. Then, she saw them suddenly stop as Augustine began to kiss the girl, pushing her, ever so slowly, towards the wall. The girl, however, was obviously uncomfortable at how things were turning out, gave a little scream and managed to struggle out of his arms.

"Don't do that to me, Augustine! I don't like it!"

"You don't really imagine, do you, that it's your scintillating conversation, your great intellect that has kept me bound to you during the last two weeks! You've been wined, dined and dressed in ways impossible for you to have imagined before meeting me, but these things all come at a price and now is the time to pay!"

With that he lunged at her, but she was a lithe, valiant, little girl and darted away from him, unfortunately towards the river. In she fell, slipping on the wet paving and shouting out in terror.

Being unable to swim, there was absolutely nothing that Marguerite could now do for her, except beg God to have mercy on her soul, but there was certainly something that she could do about Augustine, that fiend in human guise. As he approached the river's edge to watch Veronique's final moments, she rushed at him from the shadows and pushed him into the swirling water which was now being buffeted by heavy rain.

"Vengeance is sweet, Augustine, and may your soul rot in the deepest depths of hell!"

Too swollen with good living, too bloated, he was unable to fight the water – and so he died!

Later that evening, if the gargoyles that adorn the great cathedral of Notre Dame had been able to look over the parapet bordering the Seine they would have witnessed members of the city's Gendarmerie looking down upon two lifeless bodies that had been dragged out of the murky water; a tall, stout man and a young woman – she dressed in a dirty, torn, blue gown that at one time must have been quite beautiful.

Meanwhile, inside the glorious cathedral itself, sitting in the shadows of the great nave, was a shabbily dressed woman, a rosary held limply in her hand. Evening mass had finished over fifteen minutes ago, but the scent of incense still filled the air, wafting prayers to God. However, the fragrant aroma went unnoticed by Marguerite, for she too, like Augustine and Veronique, was now dead, her heart unable to bear any more of this world's suffering. The shadows had finally disappeared for her and there remained only a blazing, wondrous reality.

THE JOGGING CLUB

BY HILARY COOMBES

Overweight female joggers usually smiled at Paula. The perfectly slim ones in impeccable jogging gear never did. Jogging was akin to joining a silent club, the sort of group that dog owners belonged to automatically. Paula belonged to the overweight group.

Have I mentioned Paula before? She's a lovely lady. A little overweight perhaps, which I suppose is the starting point of our story. She's trying to lose excess pounds when we join her pounding along the beachfront one sunny Spanish morning.

Paula always stared enviously when Miss Dior passed. She had nicknamed the perfectly shaped jogger with this illustrious title because, as well as looking every centimetre a catwalk model, the smell of a million roses wafted ahead of her, and these were expensive roses it was obvious.

Ahh, that perfume aroma! It was lovely and Paula felt like running a ring around the woman just to get another whiff, not that she would have been capable of running a ring around this fit, expensively clad, woman.

Paula felt certain happiness when one or other of the women, puffing their way along the beachfront, smiled at her. It was the heartening antidote to the antipathy of forcing her body to get out of bed early. She knew that within the hour the workers and holidaymakers would be up and about and the thought of them watching her flab rise and fall filled her with dread.

The day that one of the overweight joggers thrust a piece of paper into her hand as she passed was to be a turning point in her life. A turning point that even her wildest dreams couldn't have predicted. Paula thrust the paper into her pocket and continued puffing.

Next day as she was sorting out the washing the short note fell from the pocket of her shorts. It seemed that Sue, whoever she was, was hoping to form a joggers club for the overweight and was inviting Paula to join.

Paula blushed. Surely she didn't look that fat! A little bit chubby was how she'd rather she'd put it. Well, perhaps a little more than a little bit, but at least she was trying to do something about it. Why else would she be getting up at ridiculous hours to do something she hated?

She threw the paper into the bin and buried all feelings of overweight guilt, but that was only until next day when she once more pulled on her oversize shorts and pounded the beach.

A rather large lady held her arms aloft and waved, as Paula was about to pass. "Hi, my name is Sue. Did you read my note? Are you coming tonight?"

The fog that was Paula's mind at such a ridiculously early hour struggled to think why she was expected to be anywhere that night and then she remembered the proposed overweight joggers club.

"Unum. Umm. Dunno," was the only feeble response she could muster as she endeavoured to stretch her tee shirt over the bump that was definitely not an unborn baby!

Clicking through the TV channels that night brought nothing but doom and gloom, either that or cookery programmes and they always drove her to raid the kitchen cupboard for a packet of crisps. Reduced fat of course.

As she opened the food cupboard she remembered the encounter with the morning jogger. She grimaced at the open door, 'What did she say her name was?' She realised she had said the words out loud to an empty kitchen.

Still talking to the ether, she made her way to the utility room. 'You've lost your grip girl,' she admonished herself, 'you'll be talking to the washing machine next.' She rummaged in the bin and smoothed out up the screwed up note, before glancing at her watch. She had time to reach Sue's house, just about.

Pinching her lips together she weighed up her options - a night of snacking in front of the TV. It's what lonely people do. Don't they? Eat and watch TV, or watch TV and eat. Such exciting lives! On the other hand she could meet with other slightly chubby joggers. Not a great choice really.

Then the normal fear that lived somewhere in her hippocampus kicked in. What if she was the largest person there? How embarrassing would that be!

Her alter ego quickly replied, 'No you won't be the largest. Remember the size of Sue. Go on, get yourself going or you'll be late. It'll be better than being lonely at home.'

Her alter ego won and thirty minutes later, Paula stood on Sue's doorstep pressing the doorbell. She could hear music and laughter coming from inside. It sounded more like a party than a meeting of the elephant brigade.

A large caftan clad lady opened the door. 'Come in. Come in, whoever you are. Come and join the club, we're having a great time.'

And so they were. As Paula entered the room she was greeted like a long lost friend. Her ears were attacked by loud laughter and the smell of bbq sausages assaulted her nostrils.

Some of the ladies she recognised from the morning nods and smiles that had been exchanged and she was surprised to see a couple of men in the room. Overweight men she observed.

Sue appeared from the garden. "Hello. Hello. Welcome to our little gathering."

"Sorry I'm late."

"Don't worry. I'm Sue, and you are?"

"Paula."

"Glad you could make it, Paula. We're just about to discuss how we can all become slim, young things again." Sue smiled as she handed her a hastily scribbled badge and safety pin. "We're all wearing our names; helps everyone get to know one another."

Paula pinned her name to the baggy dress that she was hiding under. She'd chosen it online, thinking that it would be flattering. It wasn't, but she quickly forgot about her bad dress choice as she became caught up in the excitement and enthusiasm of her fellow joggers.

Driving home later that night Paula felt a burst of energy and positiveness that hadn't entered her life for a very long time. Yes, tomorrow would be the start of a new chapter and one where she really was going to become stick shaped.

Morning jogs from then on became far more pleasant affairs, although Paula still didn't like getting up with the birds. The OJ Club (as the Overweight Joggers called themselves), met once a week to discuss progress and, if wished, they could be secretly weighed by Sue. It turned out that Sue was a dab hand at organising discussions about all things weight related, from good running trainers to calorie counting exercises.

On the fourth week, Sue invited Lydia, a psychologist friend, to talk to the group about making resolutions and keeping them. Lydia advised the group not to get upset because they'd had a bad day, perhaps ate too much or hadn't exercised. She said they should just put it behind them and remember tomorrow would be a new start.

Paula noticed that everyone was nodding when these words were spoken. She also noticed the puzzled faces when they were told to write down their dearest desire, suggesting this possibly might be to shed the excess fat cells. They were to kiss the paper and put it under the pillow that night before going to sleep and make sure they looked at it every night until they'd achieved their aim.

Paula thought this was plain daft and obviously Mark, who was sitting next to her, was of the same opinion if his screwed up face was anything to go by.

That night as Paula kissed the folded piece of paper and thrust it under her pillow she felt foolish and wondered why she, a grown woman, was carrying out this hocus pocus rubbish. What on earth did she hope to gain?

Nevertheless she left the paper in place and forgot all about it until a few days later when jogging along the beach.

It had become Paula's habit, once she felt safely out of sight of anyone, to incorporate a few exercises as she jogged. So flinging her arms out to the side and above her head was a regular occurrence. Singing along noisily to Abba, who was thumping out Dancing Queen through her earphones. Swirling her arms around like a mad Cossack dancer suddenly the irresistible force of her right arm met a solid almost immovable object. The unexpected jolt caught her off-guard and the next thing she knew she was spread-eagled on the sand.

Poor Paula, I wager you are thinking, but no, let me set the scene. There she was, this still slightly chubby lady sprawled face down on the sand. Standing over her was this still slightly chubby man, his red sweaty face a picture of shock and concern.

She wriggled around trying to keep some dignity as she awkwardly struggled to her knees, her back still bent over the sand.

She tried to stop coughing and spluttering from the overdose of sand that had invaded her mouth.

He hopped from one foot to the other, ineffectively outstretching and waving his arms about, wondering how to best help.

She rescued her fallen earphones and straightened up her spine, but still knelt on the sand pondering how best to stand without losing all self-respect.

His outstretched arm had now made contact with her shoulder. "Paula, I am so sorry."

Her ears registered the use of her name and she swivelled her head to glimpse the source of speech. "Mark! It's you!" Paula had thumped solid built slightly chubby, Mark and she had come off worse.

"I'm so sorry Paula." His concerned face reflected the feeling.

Paula was glad that the sand clung to her cheeks hiding their tomato red colour. "It's not your fault. I shouldn't have been flinging my arms around."

"No. No. I shouldn't have tried to overtake you."

The two OJ Club members stood and looked at each other and simultaneously broke into laughter.

"Well, it's a lucky escape that you weren't really hurt." Mark smiled, "come on, let's go for a diet coke."

And, with a smile and a nod that's how it all began. Over their drink they talked about diets and exercise, the people in the OJ Club, the speakers, in fact they chatted like long-time buddies, which was what they were about to become.

You'll be glad to know that Paula has now moved on and is not a member of the OJ Club any longer, and neither is she lonely.

Why should she be? She now has Mark beside her. Did I mention he moved in? No? I meant to. And did I mention their joint amazement when they revealed to each other what they had written on those pieces of paper they had thrust under their pillows?

You won't be surprised to learn that they had written identical words and it had nothing to do with losing weight.

You also won't be surprised when I say that their dearest desire has come true, for now they are as happy as two bugs in a rug. Two slightly chubby bugs who, when they go to sleep each night, still keep their 'dearest desire' papers side by side under the pillow.

CONSEQUENCES

BY JOHN ROSS

"They blame us and are looking for some sort of apology or they will respond accordingly."

He felt the tension level in the room increase.

"So what do you suggest?" he asked, leaning back in the black leather swivel chair and looking at his team of advisors.

As a president who had only been in office less than a hundred days he relied heavily on his advisors for guidance and, as a result, he valued their input.

At forty seven he was not the youngest president, but he was a lot younger than the last three and he was voted in on a tidal wave of need for change. However, this did leave him a little short of experience but nobody, since the cold war, had the necessary experience to handle this situation except maybe Tom Walkinshaw, the tall, sixty eight-year-old Texan who had guided him to the White House.

Nevertheless, it was not Tom that spoke first; it was Andrew Anderson the Financial Wizard who advised him on economic issues. At forty five he was younger than the president, but had the cocksure attitude that self-made multi-millionaires exude like halitosis.

"We could get our reprisal in first; hit them hard and fast before they decide what to do next."

"Are you insane, son?" Tom's Texan drawl came across the table. "We screwed up. First we need to fix it, not make it worse."

"Tom's right, much as it pains me to say it, but we got it wrong. We need to sort it PDQ before that mad Korean nukes Washington,"

Alistair McBride, ex-General US Army and now advisor on all things military, said as he stood to his full five feet, eight inches, his barrel chest straining his shirt and suit jacket. Pacing, as he did when he was thinking, he went on, "We, and when I say we I mean the marines, screwed up by not aborting that cruise missile and it landed in North Korean waters. They want an outright apology, some sort of public embarrassment I would imagine, a head on the chopping block and to be part of a review of launch and abort procedures, and they want it soon or this will escalate." His nasal Bronx accent added a certain tone to 'screwed up' and 'marines' as he paced up and down the heavily carpeted floor.

"Al, will you please sit down. You are distracting me, pacing like that." The quiet, warm tones of a deep Alabama voice came from Jolene Carter, the former Secretary of State, now supposedly retired, but at seventy one, still as sharp as a knife and a valued input to the new President on Foreign Affairs.

Al stopped and looked at the carpet, then at the chair as if he did not realise he had got up. He walked slowly back to the chair, looking at Jolene as he did so.

"Jolene, you know you look lovelier every day, I need to know your secret."

As he sat down she replied in a testy fashion, "Al, that kind of comment is no longer a compliment and is seen as sexual harassment nowadays. You need to watch your mouth, boy," a smile playing over her attractive dark face.

"OK, OK! Enough of the septuagenarian childishness," snapped the president.

"What do we do? We started this 'aggression' as he calls it. How do we get back to whatever approaches normality without losing too much face in the media?"

Tom stood up, looking very much like John Wayne in a suit as he did so.

"We can easily apologise; that costs nothing and can be spun in any way we want to. We can provide a scapegoat from the Marines if necessary, but there is no way that Kim Yung, or his cronies, are getting anywhere near our technology and processes."

McBride jumped at this, and said "The Marine Commander is pretty close to retirement anyway. We can put him out to pasture a bit early, top up his pension and make sure that he obeys orders and carries the can for the country."

"OK, so we can make an apology, we can find a scapegoat. But what happens if the Koreans want more? As president, I need a Plan B and a Plan C as well as Plan A."

Jolene turned in her chair and faced the president. "Jack, you go on TV today, you unreservedly apologise to the People of North Korea about this, explain that it was not an act of aggression but a simple accident and it is being dealt with.... end of! If the jumped-up fool with the bad haircut wants more he can keep asking. We do not crawl to dictators and bullies."

Tom and McBride nodded in agreement, but Andrew wasn't finished yet. "OK, let's do this, but for a Plan B and Plan C we can freeze all North Korean assets, stop all international aid and go proactive on the cyber front. That will scare the pants off him and get him to back down."

"Andrew, Andrew, you still don't get it do you? We were wrong, we have to apologise. All your proposing is an escalation of tension which could lead to God knows what. No, we are going to do as Jolene suggests and see what happens."

Later that day the president went on TV and made the announcement that a test firing of an unarmed cruise missile (not true) in a joint exercise with the South Korean navy went off course and, despite all best efforts to abort and self-destruct (true), the missile landed in North Korean waters where it sank without a trace, causing no casualties. The United States apologises to the People of North Korea for this accident and will take the appropriate disciplinary measures and review Cruise Missile launch and abort processes.

The announcement was heard across the world and generally ignored, but in North Korea a certain back room advisor to the Great Leader hatched a plan. In North Korea all news is heavily censored, therefore it was almost a 100% guarantee that the great North Korean people had not seen this apology from the American president. They had, of course, been told in great detail about the act of aggression from the Americans in firing a missile into North Korean waters and that, although it did not hit anything, it came very close to a fishing fleet and could have killed many people; not true but who cares?

He was Lee Yuan Dho and completely unknown to the North Korean people but, as head of Information, every word they read, every picture they saw and all TV and Radio programming was his responsibility. Like many of the party faithful he wore the traditional black Jeogori jacket and Baji trousers with soft slippers on his feet. He rarely spoke to those around him and this affectation, along with his pointed face, earned him the nick name of Jwi (pronounced Chee) - meaning The Rat - and the rat was about to have fun.

Lee Yuan Dho moved from his working desk to the editing desk in his office and started work.

A few hours later North Korean television broadcast the President of the United States effectively declaring war on North Korea by stating that the missile fired was a warning to Pyongyang and, that unless the Great Leader stepped down, the next wave of missiles would ensure that he did.

The outpouring of spontaneous, coordinated anger was evident as the party faithful ensured that all people took to the streets to protest at the aggression from the Americans and to support the Great Leader.

As this activity leaked out of North Korea, the Chinese, Russians, Iraq and others were a little confused, the Americans were furious and the United Nations was in uproar. North Korea had crossed a line that it should not have crossed, by portraying the new US president as a warmonger, claiming aggression from both US and South Korean forces that all the world knew not to be true and causing a lot of finger-pointing and paper-waving in the twenty eight embassies and consulates of the countries represented in Pyongyang. It was all getting out of control.

This was where Plan C came into effect.

Kim Pak Choe was a cook in the Presidential Palace in Pyongyang. He was also a CIA sleeper who had been in place more than 30 years waiting for the message that so far had never come. Today it did. The message was just 'NOW'.

He followed the instructions to the letter and a week later the Great Leader was dead from a heart attack, induced by Kim Pak Choe lacing the Leader's drink and food. At the same time an exiled North Korean calling himself Geu Hana, The One, went viral in North Korea (with a little help from the United States) calling for the North Korean people to unite with their South Korean cousins and become one Korea again.

The army were at a loss. The Rat, Lee Yuan Dho, could not find where this virus was coming from and could not stop it. It multiplied and re-spawned across TV, Radio, computers, mobile phones, spreading the news of the outrageous life styles of successive Leaders, the lies that had been told to the People, and how North Korea and South Korea could reunite like East and West Germany had done.

The tsunami of electronic warfare was such that the North Korean government imploded, the people rioted and the 49th parallel was reopened. It took four years, but over those four years the people of North and South became one again, redressing the balance of power in South East Asia and voting for a new president, a certain Geu Hana who was 100% funded by the American President Jack Johnson.

Having won his second term in office, Jack Johnson was watching the inauguration of Geu Hana on television in the oval office surrounded by Tom Walkinshaw, Andrew Anderson, Alistair McBride and Jolene Carter.

"Always good to have a Plan C, guys." He raised his coffee mug and toasted the group.

Note: I wrote this in the summer of 2017 when the situation between the West and North Korea was not as benign as it is currently. Tensions around global cyber propaganda, false news, manipulation of social media etc. were prevalent and it was looking like the West was losing this battle.

I wanted to create a scenario where North Korea imploded, similar to the Soviet Union, but on information not economics. By using a young U.S. President, a long term sleeper and a North Korean exile to turn the North Korean propaganda mechanism against itself appealed to my sense of irony.

The new Korean President character I gave the nickname The One in Korean as this concept of a one Korea is not unknown.

It could be argued that Korea and the world had a lucky escape albeit a highly constructed and devious one.

THE PARTY

BY MADDY PATTERN

Grace gazed at herself in the full-length mirror. What she saw pleased her for once. Although she dressed appropriately every day for work and felt confident in what she did, deep inside she didn't really feel it. The low self-esteem she knew she had was probably due to the lack of real emotional and true expressions of love from her husband, Gary. He never paid her compliments on how she looked or was thankful in how their business had thrived. At the age of 45, she now realised she needed more in her arid life...like someone who would truly love, cherish and appreciate her for who she really was.

Sighing, she glanced in the mirror again. Her red hair was brushed and gleaming, her make-up done and the lovely, low cut, halter neck, black, tan and white silk knee-length dress, which had been a wonderful buy, fitted her perfectly. She hadn't been to a party in ages and was looking forward to it. Something different from all the rest of the nights she normally spent either working in the restaurant they owned, or in the flat above.

Her thoughts were interrupted by Gary appearing from the bathroom after showering with just a towel around his waist. Without even glancing at her, he exclaimed "Ah, that was lovely!" Then proceeded to dress himself with the clothes that were laid out on the bed.

Moving to the mirror, he stared at himself then, in a rather self-satisfied voice, said, "Do I look nice? Do you like the shirt? I think it goes very nicely with my new trousers don't you?" Gary smiled.

"Yes, you look really nice." Grace said, sighing and wandering into the bathroom.

"Stop sighing; what's the matter now?" Gary snapped.

"Nothing, I'm just a bit tired. I'll feel a bit better when I've had a drink and relaxed." Grace replied, shutting the bathroom door. She heard Gary bellow, "I'm off to the pub for a drink. See you at Colin and Clare's." The flat door slammed.

Grace sat down on the toilet seat and thought "Why the hell does he think that I sigh sometimes. All he thinks about is himself, how he looks, how other people see him and he does what he likes, when he likes!" From feeling pleased at how she looked, she now felt quite disheartened and thoroughly pissed off. He could have waited for her and then they could have gone to the party together. "Shit!" She got up, brushed her teeth and left the flat.

The party was in full swing by the time Grace arrived. She had walked there and was glad she had worn her jacket as the evening had become a little chilly.

"Grace!" Clare greeted her warmly, with a kiss on both cheeks. "How nice to see you. It's not very warm is it? Come in. Where's Gary, isn't he with you?"

"I think he went to the pub first, although I would have expected him to be here by now. I expect he'll turn up soon." Grace replied.

"Oh well, you're here that's the main thing. What can I get you to drink? Colin's in the lounge and there's a table at the back of the room where you can put your present and card." Clare smiled at Grace and led the way to the kitchen.

Accepting a glass of red wine, she drifted into the lounge where she found Colin chatting with the American guy that he'd brought to the Restaurant a while back. She couldn't remember his name, only that he had two or three restaurants, one being in London. She leaned over to Colin and gave him a kiss.

"Happy Birthday Colin. I've put a present and card for you on the table with the others."

"Thank you Grace, you shouldn't have, your presence is enough." Colin said laughingly, giving her a hug.

"Where's the old bugger then? He's obviously not with you?"

"No, he said he was going to the pub first. He should be here soon." Grace laughed. "He was ready early and, you know him, can't stand still for a second!"

"Never mind, do you remember Sam? He and his son are staying with us for a few days" Colin said, turning to his left.

"Yes, I do." Grace replied as Sam grasped Grace's hand and shook it warmly.

"Let me introduce you to my son, Chris, who's over for a couple of weeks or so, helping me with some business in London."

"Hi Chris, pleased to meet you. How are you enjoying England?"

"It's great. I've been here before but always to London, never to a small English village. It's really quaint and the people are so friendly. Dad tells me that you own the Restaurant here. I'd love to have a meal there whilst I'm over." Chris said to her smiling. Grace thought, "What a nice looking boy, Josie, her daughter, might like to meet him."

She replied, "Of course. I expect your Dad will bring you for a meal. The building itself is very old, and not modern like your father's, but it has some lovely features and I love it to bits."

They chatted on for a while exchanging bits of information on their restaurants and the different cuisines they offered. In the background, pop music played and people chatted and ate. Grace could see that twit, Mick, the local builder, trying to chat up Tracy, the village bike as she was known! What a waste of space he was! Thought he was God's gift to all women and in the past had tried it on with her!

Grace, now and again, looked around for Gary. By this time it was 9.00 pm and there was still no sign of him. Where the hell was he! Sod him; she was going to enjoy herself.

Sam took her hand and led her onto the dance floor, where they danced to the music and chatted generally. She could see Tracy beginning to "perform". She had started to remove her top! God, it was early in the evening for her to be doing that, she must have had quite a few drinks, and probably had been in the pub most of the afternoon. Lordy, Lordy, you could see her bra now! Hope Clare or Colin notices soon, otherwise it'll all be off! Sam saw what was going on and laughed. Grace explained that it was Tracy's normal party trick. Poor Tracy, she thought, not the world's greatest looker but was the world's greatest exhibitionist and when she drank too much...well, anything could happen!

The evening wore on and, Grace danced, ate, chatted, and generally forgot about Gary.

It was about 11.00'ish when she was meandering back from the kitchen with another glass of wine and Mick appeared at her side. "Oh no!" she thought!

"Love of my life, where have you been? Come; let me take your glass so we can dance." He exclaimed drunkenly!

"No, it's okay, Mick, I'm just going to sit down for a while and..."

'Rubbish!" He said loudly and grabbed the glass from her hand, plonked it down on a nearby table and pulled her onto the floor. Unfortunately, it so happened that at that moment the music changed and became a slow one! Mick clasped Grace tightly round the waist, pulled her against him and proceeded to grind himself against her. She groaned inwardly, thoughts whirling round her head. She couldn't get out of this without making a scene. She eased herself discreetly away from him. "Bloody men! Where the hell was Gary? She'd just have to see this dance through. Bugger, why couldn't she just be rude and tell the twat to piss off!"

She suddenly became aware that Mick was then stroking her bottom and whispering lewd things in her ear and what he'd like to do to her. At that point she deliberately pressed down hard onto one of his shoes with a heel and, whilst he was hopping about the place, walked quickly back to the kitchen. Looking at her watch, she saw it was 11.20. Still no Gary and she had the start of a headache. She thought she'd find Clare and Colin to say goodbye and make her apologies for leaving early. As she was making her way out of the kitchen she bumped into Chris.

"Whoa, nearly knocked you down, where are you going in such a hurry?"

"Actually, I'm going home now. I've got the beginnings of a headache and have an early start tomorrow as we have a large lunch party coming. So I'm going to say my goodbye's now. Where's your dad?"

"He's on the dance floor. Some woman with bare breasts grabbed him and is hanging on to him for dear life. She looks a bit drunk to me and he doesn't look very happy!"

Grace looked across at the seething mass of dancers and could just make out Tracy, jiggling her breasts about in Sam's face whilst swigging from a glass of red wine. Oh dear, no, he didn't look very happy. Actually, it was quite funny. Quite the funniest thing this evening!

"Say goodbye to your father for me. It was nice meeting you. Don't forget to get your Dad to bring you to the Restaurant for a meal. Take care and see you soon."

After saying her farewells to various people and thank you's to Clare and Colin, Grace made her way upstairs. Turning left on the landing she went down the dimly lit corridor to the bedroom where she'd left her jacket. Walking past the bathroom she heard the sound of a flushing toilet from within. Reaching the bedroom door, she opened it and, entering, heard the bathroom door open.

Putting on the bedroom light and leaving the door ajar, she made her way over to the bed which was piled high with coats and jackets. Searching through them all, she spied her jacket underneath a large, heavy tweed coat. As she went to pull it out the room was suddenly plunged into darkness and the door clicked shut! Her first thought was that someone assumed the room to be empty, which was immediately negated by the knowledge that anyone glancing in would have seen her digging through the pile of coats.

Nevertheless, turning, she said, "Hey! Who's there?" Silence! Then, with an overwhelming jolt of shock she became aware of a presence in the room.

"What the hell's going on? Put the light on! Who are you?" She shouted.

"You can't avoid me forever." the voice said, closer now.

Despite the slurred delivery she knew who it was. Her eyes now accustomed to the dark and, helped by the slight shaft of light, which emanated through the slightly open curtains at the window. She could smell whisky and a distinctive after-shave.

"Mick, it's you, isn't it? Come on, don't be so daft! Put the light on, will you." she demanded with rising alarm.

"Come 'ere, you sexy bitch! You've been avoiding me all night, but I know what you want!" He then launched himself onto her and made a grab for whatever he could with one hand, the other fumbling with the top of her dress. Now sure of his identity and purpose Grace's mind raced for things to say, ways to placate him, play him along and gain time. She felt the ragged tear of silk and the bruising pressure of an animal paw on her breast as she was knocked off balance backwards onto the bed. Then the crushing deflation of her chest as the full, uncontrolled, weight of his torso thumped onto her before rolling away to be enveloped by the tangle of coats.

"Come 'ere, gorgeous, 'ave a feel of this!" He growled in angry frustration, disorientated and floundering in the swell of suede, cashmere, and the like. Though winded and, in pain, for a moment she was free but with his futile, heavy scrambling the bed rocked and her attempt to roll further away and get off the bed was akin to swimming through treacle. Kicking out and hoping to block his path, her elbows digging for purchase, she glimpsed the door only a few feet away, a gloomy rectangle of hope which might as well have been a mile away! Muffled oaths reached her from amongst the coats as the mattress shuddered and Mick's weight left it as he fell off the bed onto the floor on the far side.

Terrified, her heart pounding, but realising it was a chance to try to escape, she rolled off the bed...but too late! She felt a burning, wrenching grip on her ankle and, with a yelp of pain, tried to kick out at him as he dragged her towards him and back onto the bed. Trying to clutch the edge of the mattress, digging her nails in deeply, she growled in boiling fury through clenched teeth for him to get off her! She felt herself being pushed over onto her back and Mick above pinning her to the mattress with his body and legs. She could scream, try to reason, or give in? Absolutely not! However, it was too late for her to make a decision! The hard slap of his hand hit her face, fingers sinking firmly into her cheeks, his sweaty palm over her mouth, as he alternately declared his passion for her and said she was the only woman for him...followed by words of abuse.

Pulling her dress up and pushing her pants aside, she felt pure white pain as his nails scratched and tore at her skin. Her mind went blank and with tears pouring down her face as she writhed beneath him, attempting to twist her face from his grasp, she realised he was just too strong for her.

"Enjoy!" He whispered coldly, just as a blinding shaft of light fell on them from the doorway.

Then the light switch turned on and the two writhing, moaning shapes on the bed froze. Grace pushed Mick off her, jumping off the bed, pulling down her dress and rushed for the door. It was only in passing the man at the door that she realised it was Sam. She mumbled a brief thanks as she turned, horrified, disgusted and out of her mind with fear and made for the stairs.

It was at that point that Tracy, the bare-breasted dancer, lurched into the doorway and, clinging to the frame, slurred, "Herro shexy, 'ave you foun' me coat?"

Mick, still trying to pull his trousers up, spluttered outrage and obscenities at Sam for disturbing them! He too rushed past Sam pushing him aside who, in turn, knocked into Tracy, who mumbled, "Oh! It's Grach! Wha's matter?" As she hiccupped then slid slowly down the doorframe and came to rest on the plush deep pile carpet, her head resting on her chest.

Arriving back at the Restaurant, she had gone immediately up to the flat and to her bedroom, where she sank down on the bed and started to cry...her embarrassment at what had taken place and that other people had seen her together with Mick, even though nothing had happened...made her weep even more.

After a while, she stopped crying and thought, "Thank goodness, Sam had walked in!" Although what he'd thought of it all, God knows! If he hadn't come in she dreaded what the outcome might have been! She'd had a lucky escape, thanks to Sam! No doubt about that and she'd just have to face the music tomorrow! By which time it could be all around the village!

Grace left the bedroom to find her daughter. When she'd told her everything, Josie was furious and did her best to comfort her, telling her that none of it was her fault!

As they talked, Grace thought of Gary, her uncaring, errant, lying husband, with his track record of affairs and then it suddenly hit her like a thunderbolt exactly what she should do! She was going to divorce him! She would be free at last to be herself and get back to who she really was! A feeling of calm and peace descended upon her and she relaxed into her daughter's arms.

THE LITTLE SIGN

BY JENNIFER NESTEROFF

"Hey Sid, I´ve just been reading that "Who's who" magazine I took from the library:"

"Oh yeah? What´s yer want to do that for? Thought you might find yerself in it, did you?"

"Don´t be daft, Sid. I was studying it for information. There are a lot of rich toffs in it, you know, just the sort we might like to visit."

"Yer reckon? Don´t think they´d like to meet people like us, though."

"We wouldn´t be meeting them, just visiting their posh homes when they are out to have a look at what they´ve got and taking some of it when we leave. Do you catch my drift, Sid?"

"That would be stealing!"

"Now you´re with it, mate. It would be a good alternative to working down the ship-yards and I know a bloke who could help us off-load anything we took. If we are lucky we could be moving out of this dump before too long into something a little more posh ourselves. Wouldn´t you like that?"

"Yes, Bob, but it´s still stealing. I don´t think my old Mum would like that."

"Your old Mum´s been dead for twenty years, so it won´t bother her. Besides, you´ll be working your way up in the world and that would please her, wouldn´t it?"

"I suppose so, but I´ve never done anything like this before and I think I´d be scared."

"Don´t worry, I´ll be with you. I´ve had a bit of experience in this sort of thing, you know."

Sid looked at Bob with admiration. Ever since he´d started working at the ship-yard next to Bob he had considered him his friend. Some of the other men sometimes made fun of him, calling him thick head or dullard, but Bob always stuck up for him and told them to lay off. They did, too. Bob was a pretty big, hefty fellow and no-one would have wanted to take him on.

When Sid was asked to leave the room he was renting because the owner decided he wanted it for someone else, Bob said he could share his place. Sid had not been looking forward to the prospect of searching for someone willing to take him in and he felt grateful and indebted to Bob. He wished he could do something in return, although he had no idea what that could be. However, now he could at least agree to accompany Bob on this stealing venture.

Sid sighed, "All right, I´ll come. Where do you want to go?"

"I see a good address here. It´s a pent-house on top of a five story building. Sounds very smart. We could slip in dressed as plumbers when no-one is looking and take the lift up all casual and like we should be there."

"´Cept we shouldn´t."

"I said not to worry. You just do as I do."

The apartment building was situated in a lovely area with trees and flower-beds surrounding it and Sid thought it the nicest place he had been in. When he saw a squirrel hopping from branch to branch in one of the trees, he gave a loud gasp of excitement.

"Cut that out, Sid, remember you´re a plumber," snarled Bob.

"Don´t plumbers like squirrels?"

"Probably not. Now, just concentrate on the job."

As they approached the big glass main door an elegant looking lady wearing high heels and a fox fur pushed it open. Bob leapt forward and, giving her his most charming smile, held it for her.

"After you, Madam, we are here to do a job."

"I´m sure:" The lady sniffed at him and hurried on.

Sid was enthralled. "Did you see that fox? It wasn´t real, was it?"

Bob was beginning to have doubts about the wisdom of having brought Sid with him.

"No it wasn´t! Stop looking at animals and concentrate! It was lucky that we could get in so easily and there doesn´t seem to be anyone at the desk," said Bob as they looked around the lobby, "and the lift seems to be on this floor. Must have been last used by that snooty bitch who let us in."

On Bob´s instruction they sauntered across and took the lift up to the Pent-house floor. As the lift doors opened, the first thing they noticed was the little sign on the heavy oak door which said 'Beware of the cat.'

"Well, what´s that supposed to mean? Is it a joke or something? Anyway, forget it and remember what I told you, Sid. We ring the bell and if someone answers we ask if they called for a plumber and when they say "No" we excuse ourselves and skedaddle. If not, yours truly has the tools that will open a door like this."

"Really, Bob? You´re a real smart bloke, you know that?"

"I do my best, old mate."

Having ascertained that no-one was home, Bob produced a powerful looking pair of pliers from his plumber´s bag and went to work on the lock. They were soon inside.

Sid marvelled at the luxury of the large vestibule with its marble floor and chandelier hanging from the high ceiling. Beyond that a thick sea of pale grey carpet stretched away across a sumptuous living-room. Bob was pretty impressed, too, but he didn´t want to let Sid know that.

The next thing they saw was a small kitten, running toward them, mewing in welcome.

"Aw, what a cute little guy!" Sid bent down and started playing with it as it wrapped itself around his legs.

"Gawd help me, not again!" exclaimed Bob. "I´m glad we´re not robbing a zoo. At least we know all about the cat. Now leave it alone and come and help me select a few choice pieces. I think we´ll

start in the bed-room."

"Just look at that bed! It's the size of a... of a..."

"The dressing-table, Sid! We´re not here to look at beds! See what you can find in the dressing-table drawers."

At that moment they heard a soft rumbling sound that seemed to come from the vestibule.

"What the hell was that?" whispered Bob in alarm. Go and have a quiet look, Sid."

Sid tip-toed out, but was soon calling to Bob to come and see.

Sid was grinning from ear to ear.

"Now there´s your cat! Ain't he a beauty?"

Bob thought he was going to faint. There, lying in front of the entrance door was a large greyish tan creature. It was uttering a deep purring sound. The kitten was settled comfortable between its front paws.

"Is that a lioness or something?" Bob croaked.

"No, no. It´s a cougar, an American Wild-cat. Hear that purring? Cougars can´t roar, you see, they just make a sound like an ordinary cat. It sure likes the kitty, doesn´t it? That´s really sweet."

Sid suddenly noticed his stricken companion. "What´s the matter, Bob? You´re as white as a sheet. Are you afraid of the cougar?"

"´Course I bloody am! How are we supposed to get out with that lying in front of the door?"

At that moment the cougar slowly stood up and started walking up to them. Bob gave a small shriek and backed away, grabbing at Sid in the process.

"Quick! Back to the bedroom. Maybe we can shut the door on it!"

Sid did not move. He stretched out his hand to the beast and, ignoring Bob, the cougar licked it. Crooning softly to it, Sid stroked its head and tickled its ears.

"We can leave now, Bob, if you like. Better bring the bag though if you still want to look like a plumber."

Bob snatched up the bag which was still empty of loot and taking as wide a berth as possible sidled past the cougar and shot out the door. Sid gave the big cat a final pat and strolled out after him.

Outside the building Bob collapsed on a handy bench to recover his shattered nerves. He stared at Sid in amazement.

"Jeez Sid, I´ve never seen anything like that! I reckon you saved our lives!"

"It was nothing, Bob. Animals like me and I like them, is all."

Sid was happy. Happy because he´d finally been able to do something to repay Bob for his kindness and happy because he had met a cougar. And he was really happy that they hadn´t stolen anything because, whatever Bob said, he had a sneaking suspicion that his dear old Mum knew all about everything he did and was glad he hadn´t let her down.

BROTHERLY LOVE: GIDEON AND PHINEAS

BY LAWRENCE WHALLEY

Beloved, let us love one another, for love cometh of God. And every one that loveth, is born of God, and knoweth God. He that loveth not, knoweth not God; for God is love...he that dwelleth in love dwelleth in God, and God in him. (First Epistle of John 4: 7-16)

"So God is love?" The brothers were finishing their dinner before preparing for the evening performance. Gideon– known on stage as "Gideon the Gambler" – was a celebrated magician and escapologist. He liked to tell his audience just how risky each escape would be. He would emphasise how any escape was dangerous and could even be fatal. His brother Phin – short for Phineas - was not a magician; he kept Gideon's show on the road, booking hotels, arranging transport of theatrical props and generally keeping up appearances in every sort of way.

Phin was reading from a book of devotional prayers given him years ago by their mother before she passed away. She often said "It's a risky business all this escapology and, no matter how careful you are, it's always a good idea to have prayed a little to make sure everything goes to plan." Mother had been a Christian and a psychotherapist and, before finding religion, was a well-known illusionist and sometime clairvoyant.

"Gideon, y'know how we're brothers and that we'd do anything for each other?" Phin's voice was slightly submissive but on this occasion had a harder edge. "Well, don't you think it's time for me to get on stage, build up what I do? Wouldn't that be the charitable, the Christian thing to do?"

Gideon had been down this path many times and just as before he listened passively. Phin let the book fall onto his knees under Gideon's hard stare and turned to look at Gideon, straight in the eye. Gideon stared back.

"Don't be an ass, Phin. You know you don't have a talent for magic and you've never learnt the escape tricks. You don't understand the risks." Gideon wanted to appear well-intended but Phin saw it as condescending, pompous and not Christian at all.

Phin wasn't going to give up. He'd been thinking about this moment for a few weeks.

"I thought you would say that and thought I'd give you one last chance. This is it, the last time I'll ask; won't you change your mind and give me a start on stage?"

Gideon stopped smiling and glared at his brother.

"Forget it, Phin; you've absolutely no talent for stage-work. You're what you've always been, what mother said, a back-room boy, fit for cleaning and clearing up, you're hopeless. Don't get fancy ideas. You're an embarrassment already. Think how much worse it would be for both of us if people saw you messing up my act!"

Yet again they'd reached an impasse, the same point in the argument that had lasted years. Phin felt he was trapped as worse than the junior partner in his relationship with his brother and he knew too that mother was at least partly to blame. Gideon had been her favourite, held up to him as smarter, quicker and nicer to be with. Worse, he couldn't see a way out, shackled to someone who thought himself not only superior in every way but someone who needed to be totally in control. Phin waited before speaking again. So Gideon continued, but more persuasive.

"I'm not sure you're so right about mother. She said lots of things about you. Sometimes, I think she just kidded you along so you didn't feel too jealous about me."

"Bollocks" exclaimed Phin.

Gideon shouted back: "You were always her favourite because she knew you were soft in the head and she wanted me to look after you. I've carried you for years. Who do you think puts food on the table? Who pays for these hotels, buys you good clothes, all just like mine. It's me and don't you forget it, you ungrateful sod. Without me you'd be in the gutter where you belong."

Phin had heard this so many times before it no longer hurt and, anyway, this time, he had something different to say.

"Let's think" said Phin "what would mother say to us now? She was a good Christian. She wouldn't want us to fight, would she?"

Gideon smirked and moved to stand over his brother.

"I'd smash your face in any day...watch yourself, you little git!" He tapped Phin under his chin.

Phin was always frightened by Gideon's aggression and chose his words carefully before he spoke, slowly and deliberately.

"Not so clever are you? My smashed face wouldn't help you, would it?"

Gideon wasn't backing off and paused before dismissing Phin with "there's more than one way to put you in your place... Now! Get ready for work. We've a show in a couple of hours and we've plenty to do."

Like many other escapologists, time spent in preparation could make the difference between life and death. Gideon was meticulous; bondage chains that looked the part, coffins with steel false bottoms and hidden microphones. Of course, Gideon knew he couldn't rely on the theatre to provide reliable stage hands. It had to be Phil. That dim witted idiot wasn't smart enough to figure out how the tricks worked. He wouldn't spoil the show by spilling the beans because he was clueless. On balance, Gideon thought that a good thing.

Later, as Gideon was checking his stage equipment, Phin was doing his best to ruin Gideon's day. Maybe a few prayers; get forgiveness in first then hit Gideon where it hurt most – his pride! They'd dressed for work, following a well-trodden routine. Yes, they were a bit superstitious, perhaps more than most performers – mother was a clairvoyant after all! - same suit and tie. Phin always carried a raincoat – whether it rained or not and they each followed different routes to the theatre: Gideon through the stage door and Phil with his ticket for an end of row seat in the back stalls as close as possible to the gents' toilet.

This time, Phil changed his routine and stopped to buy a canister of lighter fuel, wearing a cap and heavy spectacles fitted with plain glass. A little diversion caused by the fire alarm, triggered when Gideon was trapped in the coffin – that would teach him a lesson. He would be sorry he'd bossed him around - no more humiliation, no more ridicule.

As Gideon went through his routine and had almost finished his escape from a straight jacket, Phin rose from his seat and went to the toilet. He stuffed a lighter fuel soaked rag under the nearest smoke alarm, went into a toilet cubicle and plugged in an earpiece to listen to Gideon's voice from inside the chest.

Nothing ever goes exactly to plan. That thought was very much in Phin's mind in the days after the fire. The theatre had burned all night and much of the next day. The audience had been successfully evacuated. Phin watched the TV news several times until he was sure that nobody had been injured in the fire. "I couldn't live with myself if that had happened" he'd thought. Among the fire damaged debris of the blackened shell of the theatre, he saw a fireman poke among the embers of a coffin totally destroyed by fire.

One thing he didn't anticipate was his reception by the crowd outside.

"Great show! Bet you didn't expect that" said one man.

"At first I thought it was part of the show" said another woman...we're so pleased you escaped."

"Yes." Phin murmured. "It was a lucky escape."

The TV news reporter was finishing his interview.

"That was a miraculous escape. I can't call it lucky. When will we see Gideon the Gambler again? When's the next show?"

"Oh, never! I've had too many scary moments to trust my luck again. I'm retiring, no question. You've seen the last of Gideon the Gambler. You're right it was miraculous and I'll take that as a sign from God. I will follow my mother's advice and follow a religious, a righteous path."

For good, of that Phin was certain. It had been a terrific act but nothing without him. Of course, he would try to miss his identical twin brother.

AS IF HE WASN'T THERE

BY OWEN SUTHERLAND

Shoes sharp rapping on the cabin floor

Like depth charge detonations on my grave

For I am buried in the coffin corpse alive

Trapped deep in a submarine of fear

A life support of oxygen and iron lung

A diatom who cannot speak or swim

Existing but invisible to their stethoscopes

I am drowning in tears I cannot shed

Deafened by screams no one can hear

Submerged rage beneath oceans of pain.

I am a dream in a sunken ship

A bubble of ego panting for life

A chest full of treasure love for my wife

Pieces of hate for my sinking fate

A subconscious wreck lost in a body of brine.

Don't turn the page – just one more line

Perhaps I'll feel the tickle on my toes

A life line to the blue sky's shimmer

A chance to relive the previous verse

For no one knows the next sheet's story.

A gentle current shifts my balance

Turns me softly to a pristine surface

A prefect sphere rising to the heavens

An expanding world of glowing love,

A universe at one a burning sun

A new chapter of living has begun.

HELL

BY ROSEMARY SHEPPARD

I'm only 22. I've been married almost two years and the baby, Skippy as we call him, is 22 months now. You might say it's young to be married with a baby these days, but Paul and I have known each other since we were babies, our families living next door to each other as they do. He's only six months older than me and so we grew up together. At first, when we were toddlers, he was like a brother to me but then it sort of changed and he became my boyfriend; can't remember how old we were when that happened but ever since then I've known that I would be with him for ever, and that always made me feel very secure and safe. Apparently he even told his Mum when he was seven that he was going to marry me. There's never ever been anyone else for either of us, well, except for that time I went to Blackpool with my Mum and Dad when I was fifteen but we won't go into that. I really love him and he really loves me and the baby. In fact everyone likes Paul. He'd help anyone out and he's wonderful with Skippy. He's really a smashing chap, one of the best, with a heart of gold and he's got this lovely sunny smile, well.....

He always knew what he wanted to do with his life, right from a kid. I think his Mum tried to talk him out of it but when he's made his mind up on something there's no moving him. So as soon as he could he went off and joined up and did his training. He looked so smart in his uniform. The whole street came out to see him when he came home the first time. It's like that where we live. We know everyone and they all know us, like a big family really. It was when he first came home on leave after he'd made Corporal that he proposed to me though everyone already knew that we would get married. He even went down on one knee and he had the ring and everything. It was so romantic.

The wedding was a smashing day. Our Mum and Dads being so pally, they paid for it all between them with Paul chipping in too. He said it was only right. We got hitched in the church round the corner and then had the reception at the church hall. Our Mums did the food – heaps of it there was, they were cooking for weeks, and everyone in the street was invited as well as some of his squaddy friends. They even formed a line of honour when we came out the church. I'd told him he wasn't to get too drunk on his stag night but he's no fool. He got all his mates drunk and then came home and went to bed before midnight. I had a lovely dress. The lady over the road who does dressmaking made it for me and it was like something out of a magazine. Paul said he'd never seen anyone look so beautiful. Made me cry. Makes me cry to think of it now...

There was no point in us getting our own place, him being away so much so I just moved into his room next door, after we came back off honeymoon. Seemed funny at first but at least I'd left home, as it were. I'd worked down the bakers in the High Street as a Saturday job when I was at school so after I left school I went there full time. They're nice there and I've got no qualifications or anything. Didn't seem any point when I knew that I was going to marry Paul. I can add up quite well and don't need anyone or anything to tell me what change to give etc. I'm also quite good at reading and writing. Paul always says he loves getting my letters 'cos they tell him everything that's going on in the street, and he can see it in his mind. He's got a good imagination. He's......

I fell for the baby almost straight away, but didn't find out till after he'd gone back on duty. He rang me when he got the letter and I can still hear him now, how excited he was. As it happened he was home when the baby was born so he came to the hospital with me and held my hand all the way through. I'm terribly squeamish, always have been, but he's so good and he was marvellous with the baby, changing his nappies and all and showing me what to do though how he knows all that I don't really know. I missed him so much when he had to go back but at least I had his Mum and my Mum to help out, and I was able to go back to the bakers part time which was nice.

Paul came home again at Christmas and it was just grand having the baby with the tree and the decorations and everything and Paul put on a Father Christmas outfit and pretended that the baby could talk and was making remarks about everything. How we laughed. Oh, we did!

That was the last time we were together before the incident.

It was on a Monday afternoon that we got the news. It seems that there had been an incident in Helmand Province, and Paul had been badly injured. It was such a dreadful shock for us all but they said that his life was not in danger. He would be flown home as soon as possible and would have the best treatment available. I was beside myself with worry and wondered how long it would be before he was better and able to get back to normal.

A few days later when he was back in the UK hospital I was asked to go in and see the Doctors. We all went; Paul's parents and my parents, and I had the baby too. The hospital was a fair journey away and it took a while to get there. It was all a bit cramped in the one car but we were all laughing and talking and the time soon passed. We were all looking forward to seeing Paul, and finding out what had happened. We'd no sooner set foot in the hospital building than we saw a young man coming towards us. Well, how I wasn't sick I don't know. He looked like that bloke on the telly sometimes, that Simon Weston. I always had to look away when he and others like him were on and, as a child, I'd even had nightmares about people with burned faces and woken up screaming. This young man was even worse, like something out of a horror film and I clutched my Dad's hand and he murmured something about the poor sod's life being over or something.

We were shown into an office and this Doctor came in and sat down and he looked very serious and I began to get frightened and clasped the baby to me so tightly that he started to cry. Then the Doctor told us. It seemed that there had been a raid on Paul's camp and he had been helping to save men in his squad when he got badly burned. The right side of his face had been almost entirely burned away and both his hands. His right eye was gone and his left eye was damaged but he would get the sight back in it in time. The doctor said that treatment had already begun to try and salvage as much of his face as possible and that in time, after lots of operations, they would be able to rebuild it and do something with his hands too. In the meantime he would be in hospital for a number of weeks and then go home to convalesce and recuperate in the bosom of his family. I don't remember much more after that. I think I sort of passed out. I know the doctor said we could see Paul then and they sort of almost carried me out of the office and along all these corridors, and finally we got to this ward and Paul was in a side-room all covered in bandages and heavily sedated. He hardly knew we were there and the baby was crying and had to go outside. That was last week.

Since then no-one has said very much to me about it though I know they are thinking about Paul all the time. His parents look like they are in some sort of trance and my Mum is pretty much the same. My Dad just put his arm round me and said that I would have to be strong and things would work out but he just doesn't understand how I feel, none of them do. When I go to work the other women give me sad smiles and look embarrassed and even the customers avoid looking straight at me. It's dreadful. I want to scream the place down.

I know that this is when I should be strong for Paul, be a true wife to him and be there for him like he had always been for me, but I can't do it. I know I can't. I can't face having to look at his face, at his hands, or what used to be his face and hands. I will be physically sick, I know I will. I can't face the thought of lying alongside him with him like that, having him touch me. The very idea makes me gag. I love him so much but all I can see is that poor chap in the hospital and I know I can't do it. I simply can't. With his one good eye he will see me flinch when he comes near me and how can I hurt him like that, when he has been hurt so much already. Even if they can do something at the hospital, he will never be as he was before. His lovely sunny face is gone forever and wherever we go, people will stare and then look away and say things about him behind their hands and I shall want to run away and hide.

We have all our lives ahead of us but what will they be now but lives full of pain and horror? It's all so unfair. Why did this have to happen to him, to me I feel so terribly sorry for him, I do, but that doesn't stop me dreading the future if I stay....But what alternative do I have.? My entire life is here. I don't have anywhere else to go. I'm trapped. If I turn my back on Paul I will be turning my back on my family, his family, everyone I know. They will all hate me and rightly so. I have no qualifications, no way of making a life apart for me and the baby and how could I take the baby away from his father who has already lost so much.

There must be a way out of this nightmare, there just must be, but the only one who could advise me and tell me what to do is the very person I can't ask.

Dear God! I beseech you. Help me, please, for I feel that I truly am in Hell.

I'm only 22.

Note: I don't know where the idea for this came from. Our subject was Hell and this is my interpretation. Unlike the other stories this does not include a lucky escape but depicts, in contrast, a situation which appears to offer no escape at all...

"VENUS"

BY DOT GARRETT

Leo loved his name, it commanded respect and had helped him confidently achieve his goals in life.

He gazed at the view across the river from his office window, the floor to ceiling windows reflecting the rays of the sun as they hit the passing boats. At times they dazzled him as he stood while lost in his reverie.

He had not always been named Leo; the young boy called Colin had been born into poverty to a drug-addicted mother. She had not been capable of raising him properly, but had slipped under the radar of the authorities. Colin had lived by his wits and as soon as he was able to leave home he had changed his name and vowed never to go back.

He had been ruthless in business and now owned a large finance company in the city. He looked down on his peers and regarded women as inferior beings, labelling them as weak, as he judged his mother had been. Leo never stopped to think about his mother's circumstances, of how she had become dependent on drugs or what had happened to her since he left. When he did think of her it was with loathing and disgust.

This opinion became his rule for all women. He felt superior and could never be equal to them. Therefore he could never love one. He sorted out women of beauty; his idea of what he thought perfect was constantly changing as he searched for the ultimate goddess to accompany him to the many official events he had to attend; also to his bed, where his deviant practises usually ensured he never saw them again.

The intercom buzzed on his desk.

"Yes, Emily, what is it?"

"Just to remind you about the awards ceremony tonight! Do you want me to contact the agency?"

He sighed. "Yes, please, Emily, and tell them to send someone who doesn't talk too much this time."

"I will, Mr Davenport."

As he settled back in front of his computer, Leo didn't give much thought to whom might turn up to accompany him to the dinner that evening. The agency had strict instructions on how to vet his escorts. As long as she was beautiful and didn't ask too many questions he would be happy. Well, he convinced himself, he was happy as he pushed the nagging thoughts out of his mind. They had been creeping in more and more often lately, but he knew he didn't want anyone to share his life; he had fought too hard to achieve what he had to allow that to happen. The fear that anyone might stake a claim on any of it was too ridiculous to consider.

However, he had felt lately that something was missing from his life – someone who would really care for him. He shook the thoughts away; he must be strong. "Be careful what you wish for," he lectured himself.

That evening he stood with a dazzling beauty on his arm and he struggled to remember her name. Annabel, that's right, he had already judged her as another empty-headed bimbo.

He concentrated on the many men that came to shake his hand and talk business; while their partners murmured and discussed dresses, he assumed.

His confidence grew when he realised that he didn't have to seek out anyone important for they all were queuing to talk to him. He glanced around occasionally and his gaze settled on a startling woman. She appeared to be on her own and his eyes followed her to see whom she might be accompanying. He noted she was approached by a particularly important banker and they were deep in conversation, but as he stared she looked up and staring straight at him, she slowly winked.

The vision was dressed all in black, a close -fitting, shimmering dress that clung to all her curves and voluptuous breasts. She wore high-spiked heels and her glossy, black hair was clipped to one side cascading around her shoulders. The deepest red lipstick highlighted her seductive lips and Leo was mesmerised.

When they were all summonsed to the dining room Leo could not help but seek her out; he scanned the tables nearby and realised she was seated next to one of the CEO's of a leading bank. Again, she saw him staring and gave a sexy smile aimed his way.

"What am I doing?" he wondered as he tried to listen to what was being said around him, but he knew he had to find a way of meeting her.

Leo did not feel guilty that he ignored Annabel for most of the evening; after all she was being paid handsomely for her services, but as they joined everyone in the ballroom after the meal he knew he would not want to pay for extra services tonight.

As they glided around the dance floor Leo noticed the woman. She was standing watching him from near the outside doors. After the dance he excused himself and went to find her. As he approached the patio doors he could not see her and looking all around he wondered if she had left. Something drew him to the outside and, as he searched, even the air felt sultry.

He saw the soft glow of a cigarette burning and, turning in that direction, found her sitting by a bower. Her long, sexy legs were crossed and her gown had opened, a long slit nearly reaching her thigh.

"Come and sit by me – I have been waiting."

Leo hesitated; he had not felt out of his depth for so long and he didn't know how to deal with these feelings.

"Sorry, I have to return to my partner."

He turned to go, trying to regain control but she laughed, it was a mocking laugh and Leo suddenly felt a rage fire inside him. He swivelled round and stepped towards her. She did not flinch. He was used to people backing down to his every mood, so he suddenly stopped, looking deeply into her eyes. She smiled that soft, sexy smile again and patted the seat next to her.

"You know you want to," she said.

As he sat she took a long draw on the cigarette and slowly blew the smoke in his face, then abruptly she threw the cigarette away and leaning into him she kissed him.

Against his will he felt desire rising and as she kissed him again her tongue darted into his mouth and she gently fondled his thigh. He felt himself sinking into the pleasure he was feeling, but just as suddenly she pulled away. Before he could regain his composure she had pressed a small card into his hand and stalked away.

Straightening up, Leo tried inconspicuously to return to the ballroom. As he searched for Annabel, he also frantically looked around for the woman, but it seemed they had both left.

The next day Leo was sipping his early morning coffee, as he studied the card that was in his hand. It was black and shiny in colour with just a gold letter V and a telephone number printed on it.

He was never usually indecisive, but he had a feeling that if he rang V it could be a life changing move and he was not sure he wanted his life to change. As the morning wore on he could not get her out of his mind and that decided him – he had to meet her again and get her out of his system.

At 3 o'clock he rang her on his mobile but there was no reply. He tried again at 4.00 and then again at 5.00. That was when he realised he never did the chasing and decided he would not ring her again. Just then his phone rang.

"Hello, Leo, you wanted me?" she purred.

"Um, yes…. Yes, I want to meet you again. Are you free this evening?"

"Not until 9 o'clock, I have an earlier appointment, but you can come then"

She recited an address and Leo quickly made a note of it.

"You have me at a disadvantage; I don't even know your name."

"Last night you met Vanessa," she laughed and hung up.

Leo stared at the phone and again wondered what the hell he was getting into, but he just couldn't get Vanessa out of his mind.

He rang the bell at a very smart apartment block in the centre of town. She buzzed him up to the penthouse.

He carried a bunch of pure-white roses and, as she answered her door, she smiled.

"Beautiful, but I prefer red roses"

Leo followed Vanessa into a low-lighted living room with music softly playing; he walked over to the windows and admired the panoramic view with the lights twinkling in the town below.

"Come and sit here!" Vanessa held a glass of champagne out to him.

Taking a deep breath he did as he was told.

"What do you want from me?" asked Vanessa.

"I don't know. I shouldn't have come, but I couldn't get you out of my mind."

She smiled. "Well, you can sit here with Vanessa or you could join me in the bedroom and meet Venus."

"Who is Venus?"

"Venus is the woman of your fantasies, and she is the reason you came here tonight. But I warn you, Venus cannot be tamed or owned. If you submit, then you will be her slave until she lets you go. Are you ready for this? Are you man enough?"

Leo was entranced and knew he had finally met his match in a woman.

He just nodded as Vanessa led him to her bedroom.

She sat in a crimson and gold chair and told him to take off all his clothes, then ordering him to lie on the floor before handcuffing him to the bottom of the bed. She left the room and, again Leo had doubts as to what he was doing, but before long she was back. He opened his mouth in awe.

"Meet the woman of your dreams; I am Venus." Vanessa stood over him. She was wearing thigh length, shiny boots of black leather, a black Basque with a black-fur coat over her shoulders and she was holding a whip. She leant over him and unlocked the handcuffs, brushing his face with her long hair.

She ordered him to kiss her boots while he knelt on all fours. She struck him with the whip when he raised his head. Venus commanded him all night to her will and, for the first time, Leo felt a joy and a passion he had never felt before. He couldn't get enough of this dominatrix.

When he finally left he was bruised and sated and he knew that this is what he had been waiting for.

He visited Venus as often as she would allow and allowed her to degrade him to whatever degrees she wanted.

He knew he was becoming obsessed with her but couldn't stop. She controlled his mind and body and also his wealth, he could deny her nothing.

It had been over a year that he had been visiting Venus when he suggested they shared a home, he wanted her all to himself and couldn't bear to think of her seeing other men as he suspected she still did.

Venus just laughed "No man will ever own me or possess me."

"But, I think I love you, I can't live without you."

She just smiled but that evening she cut their session short and said she had a meeting.

Not daring to question her after his earlier outburst, Leo left.

The next day he realised he didn't want to risk upsetting Venus. He hadn't arranged to see her that evening, but he had to explain that he wanted her under any conditions.

He drove to her apartment, but there was no answer. He phoned and it went to voicemail; he begged her to return the call but all to no avail, no matter how many times he tried.

The days turned to weeks and Leo realised he had lost her. Not matter how he searched and asked about Vanessa, it seemed she had disappeared into thin air.

In his despair he tried to persuade himself that he had had a lucky escape – after all it was he who called the shots and he should have the power to decide when it ended. However, deep down he secretly wondered if karma had dealt him his just deserts; perhaps he needed to consider his behaviour towards women in the future.

Leo had to resort to using the agency again for escorts for official functions and one evening he realised he recognised the woman on his arm. It was Annabelle; she smiled sweetly and asked if he had found what he was looking for.

Looking at her with new eyes, he wondered how much she knew.

"Do you know Vanessa by any chance?"

Annabelle shook her head "I knew a woman once, but Venus was her name; she was a goddess, but she has gone now."

Then she smiled and slowly winked at him as she disappeared into the crowd.

Note: The subject for our writing group assignment was "Venus was her name". I immediately thought about songs with Venus in the title. My favorite song was "Venus in Furs" by Velvet Underground and I apologise for lifting the lyrics "shiny boots of leather". I have found myself often thinking of song lyrics when writing and they are a great source of inspiration.

A TALE TO TELL

BY LAWRENCE WHALLEY

Betty turned slowly in her bed. Half awake, she sensed her husband's presence alongside her. Her hand smoothed the familiar space where he had so often lain. She knew he wouldn't be there; he'd died nearly six months ago. His presence was somehow reassuring, like a visit from an old friend who didn't want to be too much trouble.

At first, his visits had alarmed her; sometimes Betty thought she was going mad. Should she tell anyone? She would be locked up, put away. In those early days, she almost believed that he was somewhere in the house. Acceptance that his visits existed only in her imagination came slowly but did nothing to diminish the physical pleasure she felt when she knew he was still around.

Listening outside his hideaway, Carol's old bedroom, the muffled sound of his shuffling about and the odd chuckle didn't worry her at all. Strange, she thought, how a man who worked as gentleman's tailor all his life should build radios in his spare time. She never saw the connection. Standing by the closed door to his hobby room, she half-imagined the crackle of the shortwave radio as he tuned in to some distant station, relaying an unintelligible language across thousands of miles. Wherever he is now, wouldn't it be wonderful to hear his voice again, to hear him sing as he busied himself around the house.

Downstairs in the kitchen, she set the table for two.

His framed picture was facing her across the table propped up on his placemat. She was very fond of this studio portrait taken to promote his singing career in 1966. Sadly, he was unlucky to be born with an exceptional tenor voice just when there was little interest in romantic crooners of jazz standards.

Carol took her by surprise in the kitchen.

"I didn't hear you come in...now you're here would you like some tea?" Betty pecked her daughter's cheek very gently and squeezed her hand.

"You left the door on the latch again...How many times must I tell you? Was it locked last night?" Betty tried to look cross but found herself smiling at Carol.

Mother and daughter sat at the kitchen table, drinking tea and chatting about the neighbours.

"That new woman upstairs was down here again. She says this place is too big for me and thinks I should look for somewhere else." Betty became tearful. "I can't move out... We've been here for ever...I don't know anywhere else...Can she really get the council to throw me out?"

Betty watched from the window as Carol drove away. It was true what she said. She couldn't live anywhere else. No 2, Bessie Braddock Court was all she had ever known since her marriage. She looked up and down the empty street. The postman had been and gone; a Tesco delivery van pulled up and was soon away. She thought she might take a walk before lunch, up to Keir Hardie Park or maybe a bus ride into town. She decided on a walk; it would be less trouble than anything else.

Her street was empty by day, just parked cars and delivery vans. Out on the pavement she turned towards the park, past the care home and took the last opening to the right by the dog pound. The barking had never bothered her though she'd heard neighbours complain. Once, when she'd asked her grandson about the council van that came up past her window as regular as clockwork, he'd told her it was removing the dogs that had not been wanted and put down. That was an unpleasant thought and made her hurry on into the park.

Back in bed again, same routine. "This time," she said to herself," the front door is properly locked. Carol won't be going on at me again!"

In the quiet of her room she drifted somewhere between sleep and wakefulness. Carol was a little girl again, on a swing in the park where she'd walked that morning. The crying sound, more of a whimper really, became louder and more insistent. "What is that? It's not my Carol is it? It's my imagination playing tricks again…I'm not going off my head…what is it?"

Downstairs, the sound was louder and easily located outside her front door. She looked through the spy hole: nothing. She switched on the outside light and looked again: nothing. Checking the door chain, she unlocked her door and peered bravely through the narrow space.

A small dog was crying on her doormat. Its fur seemed sodden in the rain and she could see it was shivering. Betty shut the door and locked it again. The crying continued. Betty was at a loss. What should she do? She opened her door again, unhooked the chain and stood over the little dog. Their eyes locked, the dog stood up. Betty moved inside and without a sound the dog came into her house.

"This dog has escaped from the dog pound and I must take it back." She thought, an old towel and the dog looked better already. There was no collar, the dog was a "he" and she didn't know what to do. She shared her predicament with the dog. It was pointless, she understood that much, to ask a dog for an opinion but she carried on anyway. "You really are a bonny little chappy" she said at one point, and he responded by wagging his tail and licking her hand. "I suppose I'll keep you…I think I'll call you 'Chappy' because you're a very happy chappy and you'll make me happy too."

"You'll need a lead and a proper place for him to sleep." Carol was like her dad, organised and practical. "You'll need dog bowls, dog food and we will need to take him to the vet." Carol was lovely but she did go on a bit. "And you'll need to walk him regularly – whatever the weather." Carol was getting on Betty's nerves. "We can pick most of this stuff up at Sainsbury's. That reminds me, you'll need to pick up his poo so you'll need poo-bags...what a lovely time you're going to have!"

Betty followed Carol's advice to the letter. That was until Chappy came looking for her one night and, without an invitation, jumped on her bed, curled up and fell asleep by her side. "Funny thing," she thought, "he's lying where my husband should be. I wonder if he minds Chappy lying on top of him."

Their walks to the park soon became a daily occurrence. People who had once passed her by now spoke to her or, more often, to her dog. One lady told her that Chappy was a Manchester terrier. Another that he was a cross between a Border and a Yorkshire Terrier. Betty told them she thought he was mostly Dachshund. Carol's boys came around more often saying they wanted to walk the dog. Chappy always slept for an hour or two after that.

"That woman from upstairs been at the door again" Betty told her daughter. "She wants me to swop houses with her daughter who's got three kids. Says it's immoral for me to have two bedrooms when I only need one...can she force me out? She says she can."

Carol could see how upset her mum had become. "There's nothing she can do. You're managing fine. There's nothing anyone can do to force you out of what's been your home for nearly forty years." Carol felt so certain of that. She went on about plans for the weekend. "You know," she said to her mother "ever since Chappy arrived, we've been planning our weekends around what he would like to do...its ridiculous! If it wasn't for the boys I wouldn't bother."

Betty looked puzzled. "But you said you liked it. You said Chappy kept them off their computer screens."

Carol was laughing. "Well there is that too, I suppose...his paws are too big, otherwise he'd be on Facebook!"

Betty unlocked the door and peered through the gap held by the chain. "Are you the tenant here?" A shortish woman with a clipboard was outside. "I'm Jane Lawson from the council. This is my badge. Can I come in?"

Betty unhooked the chain and led her visitor into the kitchen. Chappy didn't bark. He looked warily at the visitor then curled up on his bed.

"I see you have a dog. Is this your dog? Does he live here permanently?"

Betty described how she'd found Chappy on her doorstep in the rain and how she couldn't decide what to do but now he was an important part of her life.

Jane Lawson listened without showing any feeling. "I think you know the dog escaped from the dog pound. One of the girls who works there has seen you walking with it."

Betty felt defensive. "He's a he not an it" she said "and they can't have him back. He's mine now and if they can't look after a dog properly there's no reason for me to give him back."

Jane Lawson interrupted quickly. "Oh no Betty that's not why I'm here. There have been complaints. Someone has seen your dog and reported it – sorry him – to the council. Your tenancy agreement is explicit 'no pets'. Your dog must go."

Betty was dumbfounded. "What tenancy agreement? I've lived here forty years, seen dogs come and go from here. Never a peep from the council."

Jane Lawson stood up. "I must go. All tenancy agreements were revised four years ago. Your husband signed his copy and returned it to us. Now I really must go. But before I do I must say that dog has to go or you'll lose your tenancy. Can you understand how important that is?"

Betty nodded quietly. "What will happen to poor Chappy? What can I do?"

Jane Lawson was in the hallway, hand on the latch. "Oh, I've checked. All you need to do is take him back to the dog pound. They'll be expecting him."

It was raining again. Chappy thought he was going for a walk and was pulling on his lead even before Betty opened the door.

Carol had been in a hurry. "We'll discuss it at the weekend when we're not so busy."

But Betty felt terrible. "This is something I must do and the sooner the better." Betty had changed her shoes and pulled on her old raincoat. The rain didn't bother her as she walked to the end of the road and stopped at the dog pound. For the fifth time, she waited a while and then, pulled by Chappie went through the Park Gates. Just one last time, she thought, as the rain dripped through her hair and onto her neck.

"That woman bothering you again?" Carol was on her high horse. "I've a good mind to go upstairs and tell her I'll report her as a public nuisance – intimidating an old lady like that!"

Betty was not calmed by Carol's annoyance. "It's not her I'm worried about. I can't bear the thought of the dog pound and that van going past every week. He could end up in there."

Carol opened her handbag." Look, mum, I can go through it again if you like. We've looked into it and you've agreed. You've exercised your right to buy. The council have accepted and nobody can force you out when you own your own home."

Once more, Betty looked at the papers Carol had taken from her handbag. "But who'll pay for it? I don't have £28,000!"

Carol found herself going around in a circle. "Mum, I've explained all that. I'll pay most of it. Your rent will cover council taxes. We all win. You get to own this place with a market value well over £100,000. Stop worrying. Everything will be alright."

Chappy looked up from his bed and then, very unusually went upstairs when it wasn't even bedtime. Carol found him sitting by her old bedroom door. "Now, just what are you up to, little fella?" She thought she heard the sound of a short-wave radio from inside her old room, shook her head and went downstairs.

Chappy waited a while and then followed her into the kitchen.

HILARY COOMBES

Hilary says that she has always written and always wanted to be published, but added 'if you've never published anything you don't know how difficult this is and how much work is involved do you?'

Her success started with a couple of magazine articles a lifetime ago and developed from there to short stories and eventually full-blown novels.

She was born in the South West of England, but now lives between the Costa Blanca and Oxfordshire. She says that she adores both her countries, which is probably why they often feature in her writing.

She has won several writing awards, two of which she is particularly proud (probably because of their Spanish connections)- the 2015 Spanish Radio international short story competition, and the 2017 Ian Goven Award

Having been a member of Moraira- Teulada U3A writing group for many years, she says that the writing community are one of the loveliest bunch of people you could hope to meet, and she encourages anyone with a desire to develop creative writing to get in touch.

You can find out more about her books on her website:

http://www.hilarycoombes.com

Or on her Amazon page:

https://www.amazon.co.uk/s/ref=nb_sb_noss_2?url=search-alias%3Daps&field-keywords=hilary+coombes

DOT GARRETT

Dot was born in Essex and has lived in Moraira for the last 21 years.

She is currently the U3A Creative Writing group leader and can't quite believe that she is accepted as a writer, after leaving school at the age of 15 with zero qualifications she has constantly surprised herself through life. This life has been, on reflection, quite varied and Dot is currently trying to find time to write a novel based on her memoirs!

Although she misses her family in the UK she always appreciates the love and support received from such a creative group.

VONNIE GILES

Vonnie is the author of Acid Rain and Tightly Bound, two books of short stories based on the world of the weird.

They are published by U P Publications and can be obtained from the publisher and from Amazon. The books are also available in a Kindle version.

Vonnie, born and bred in Tewkesbury, has been living in Spain for thirty years and as well as being a long term member of the Creative Writing Group she is also a faithful member of the U3A Classical Music Group led by Geoffrey Shean.

JENNIFER NESTEROFF

Jennifer Nesteroff was born in Australia, but left there to travel when she was twenty-one. She has lived in England, Holland and Spain. She and her husband, Peter, have two children, a daughter who lives in Holland and a son in Australia.

She has been a member of the U3A Moraira Creative Writing Group for several years. Eight of her stories appeared in the book 'Picked and Mixed' which was published by UP Publications. She writes both serious and humorous stories, but enjoys writing humorous ones more.

MADELEINE PATTERN

Madeleine moved to Spain 14 years ago with her husband (who very quickly became her ex-husband...see the story "The Letter" that brings into play experiences of her marriage to him & why she divorced him! The rest of the story is fiction). Having made a life for herself here & made good friends, she had a relationship with someone for 8 years but, unfortunately, he had to return to the UK because of lack of work. He and she remain good friends. Madeleine had written poetry in the past and started writing a novel some years ago, which one day she might finish! In 2015, she moved from her villa to an apartment, which is when she joined the U3A & became a member of the group. Writing short stories is something she has come to enjoy doing...it draws on her imagination, life experience and being part of a group, which she thinks is amazing.

JOHN ROSS

John was born in Edinburgh, Scotland. Educated in Edinburgh, met his wife there, married there and then moved to several places in the UK with his employer before moving to the Middle East and eventually retiring to Moraira with his wife Elaine and two cats.

They have two sons, three grandchildren and at the time of writing another on the way. John got back into creative writing when he retired to Moraira having given it up several decades before. He is a qualified PADI Dive Master, plays golf and enjoys cooking, reading, travel and history.

ROSEMARY SHEPPARD

Rosemary is married to John and they have lived in Spain since 1999. She has enjoyed writing for as long as she can remember, mainly with the intention of making people laugh - something which she seems to be fairly successful at doing.

Over the years she has started at least three novels but just doesn't have the application needed to finish them so a short story is an ideal project for her.

She has belonged to the U3A Creative Writing Group for several years and finds it stimulating, informative and great fun.

CAROLYN SIMS

Carolyn has lived for three years on the Costa Blanca, having spent the previous fifteen years in France, USA, Canada and the U.K. She enjoys the discipline of writing to a given theme under 2500 words. She has no pretensions to being a serious author, so the Creative Writing Group offers her the opportunity to create imaginative short stories often based on her family and friends.

Carolyn has been married for 52 years to Philip; they have two children, six grandchildren and one great grandchild.

ROBERT WEBB

Robert was born in the heart of London at Charing Cross, but apparently at the hospital, not the station! A grammar school boy from the 1960s, he always enjoyed art, music, reading and creative writing, but when it came to entering the world of work, earning a living came first. He worked in job roles which he describes as "less than inspiring", and in the 1990s took time out from his career to study English Literature at degree level, where his interest in creative writing was rekindled.   After graduating, the demands of work once again meant that writing still took a back seat, however.

Now retired and living in Benitachell, Robert has enjoyed creating short stories for the U3A writing group and aims to concentrate on longer pieces with a view to getting into print one day. As well as short stories, he would also like to work towards completing a full-length novel.

The writers he enjoys most include DH Lawrence, Orwell, Steinbeck, Hemingway and, more recently, Philip Roth, John Irving and Anne Tyler. Robert is also a fan of crime / detective novels by writers such as Robert B. Parker (TV's Spenser and Jesse Stone) and Michael Connelly (TV detective, Harry Bosch).

LAWRENCE WHALLEY

Lawrence was born in Lancashire, received medical training in Newcastle and spent all his adult life in Scotland. He retired in 2008 from a career in academic medicine when writing was a large part of the job. He spends half the year in sunny Spain where he stepped up to the U3A creative writing group to wander among the imaginative story-telling of likeminded people. His stories selected for inclusion here were much improved by comments received from the group. Lawrence lives alone with two dogs. He has two former wives, three daughters, two step daughters, one step son, six grandchildren, and two step grandchildren. He struggles to remember their birthdays.

31087378R00179

Printed in Poland
by Amazon Fulfillment
Poland Sp. z o.o., Wrocław